EDMUND+OCTAVIA

The Dulcie Chambers Museum Mysteries

by Kerry J Charles

An Exhibit of Madness
(Previous Title: Portrait of a Murder)

From the Murky Deep

The Fragile Flower

A Mind Within

Last of the Vintage

A MIND WITHIN

A Dulcie Chambers Museum Mystery

Kerry J Charles

EDMUND+OCTAVIA

Cover Image: *David*, 1501-1504, Michelangelo di Lodovico Buonarroti Simoni. This image is in the public domain.

ISBN: 0989457672
ISBN-13: 978-0-9894576-7-5

For Noah, because you see the world differently.

CONTENTS

CHAPTER ONE

It wasn't a face. He never saw a face. It was only curves and lines and colors that seemed to move around each other and grow, from the top of the canvas down to the bottom. It never started with an oval, then eyes, perhaps a mouth next, the tricky nose placed in between, as artists throughout the millennia had painted portraits. His always began at the top and worked its way down. It wasn't a face. Not to him.

Dulcie watched in amazement. He began with one swooping stroke. A lock of brown hair starting at the top, sliding half way down the canvas. Then another, and another. Then eyebrows… eyes beneath. A nose… ears… mouth. Chin, neck, shoulders…. Each was perfectly rendered before he moved on to the next.

She had entered the room only ten minutes before and he had barely glanced at her, yet it was as though she was looking into a mirror. He had captured her likeness so perfectly, so exactly. How was it possible?

"Has he seen me before?" Dulcie asked without taking her eyes off his work. The woman beside her shrugged her shoulders.

"Possibly. He has been to the art museum. He might have seen you in a newspaper article as well. Perhaps." She had a soft accent. French, or possibly French-Canadian.

The young man abruptly put down his brush and walked to the window. He was done.

"What now?" asked Dulcie quietly.

"Now it goes in the stack with the others," the woman gestured toward the corner of the room. Dozens of paintings were propped against the wall, mostly portraits, from what Dulcie could see. Many looked as though they were of the same person: a middle-aged man. "Unless you want it?" the woman asked Dulcie.

"May I?"

The woman shrugged again.

"I feel as though I should ask him," Dulcie said.

"You can try, but I'm afraid you won't get a response," the woman replied. It was not said unkindly, simply as a matter of fact.

Dulcie crossed the room and stood beside the young man. She knew that he was fifteen. She didn't look at him, she simply stood beside him and looked out the window as he did. He was still, silent. At last Dulcie said softly, "May I have the painting of me?"

Nothing. Then, in one slow gesture, he turned his hand and opened it so that the palm faced up.

"Thank you," Dulcie whispered.

The other woman in the room had not noticed. She was attending to her work, making sure that the room was in order, that the young man would have what he needed. Dulcie couldn't know that his simple gesture was the first communication that he had made in months.

∛

"What the heck is that?" Dulcie's brother exclaimed as he entered Dulcie's office in the Maine Museum of Art. He pointed to an odd assemblage of bottle caps. Thousands of them were stuck together, forming a human-sized Statue of Liberty.

Dan Chambers never minced words, which always amused Dulcie. However, she knew his reaction would be common among visitors viewing the new exhibit.

"It's called Outsider Art," she said.

"Never heard of it."

"I wouldn't imagine that you had," she said. "Most people haven't. It comes from the French *art brut* which means raw or rough art. It can mean a lot of things, but it includes art made by people who aren't professional artists, such as indigents, people with brain traumas, the insane… even children. Basically, they're compelled to create, usually beyond a level that we would consider normal."

"Wow," Dan simply stated. He hadn't taken his eyes of the statue. "What's it stuck together with?" he asked, leaning in for a closer look.

"Gum," Dulcie said.

"You mean like gummy glue kind of stuff?"

"No, I mean chewing gum," she replied.

Dan instantly pulled back. "Gross!"

Dulcie shook her head. "Well, it's completely hardened by now, silly. The thing is at least five years old. The police found it in an abandoned warehouse outside of Boston. They knew there was a homeless guy living there for a while. They didn't bother him since he never caused any trouble, they said, but they had no idea he was making this," she nodded toward the statue. "When he died on the streets, they went to the place where they knew he'd been staying and found the statue."

Dan was more appreciative standing a few feet back. "I wonder how long it took him to make?"

"Good question! I have so many questions about it, which we'll never have answers for, unfortunately."

Dan crossed the room and sat in the chair by his sister's desk. He was still amazed that she was the director of the entire museum. She definitely had the brains in the family, although he had his own kind of common-sense wisdom. "So is this the beginnings of a new exhibit?" he asked.

"Yes, and I'm pretty excited about it. I'm hoping that it will get people thinking about what really defines art. We always assume it's Leonardos and such. But it's much more basic to the human psyche than that. It's expression and communication, and probably a lot of other things."

"Thank you for the lecture, Dr. Chambers," Dan said with mock applause.

She smirked at him. "Someone needs to broaden your horizons," she said looking back at her computer. "I've got a lot of pieces coming in over the next couple of days," she said, scrolling through images. "It's gonna get busy."

Dulcie stood up quickly, making her brother jump. "Hey," she said, "come down to my car. I want to show you something."

They left her office, walking by the museum's front desk. Dan winked at Dulcie's assistant, Rachel. She giggled. Dulcie rolled her eyes at her brother. "Stop that!" she mouthed.

In the parking lot, Dulcie opened the back of her ancient Jeep Wrangler. She had known for some time that she should get a new vehicle, but couldn't bear to part with it. Not yet.

"What do you think of this?" she asked, pulling out the portrait of herself.

"*Aaahhhh*!" Dan yelled in fear, putting his hand over his heart in mock terror at the sight. Dulcie swatted him. "Sorry. Had to," he grinned. "But seriously, it's definitely you. When did you sit for a portrait?"

"That's the weird thing. I didn't. This is another example of Outsider Art. A young man, actually more like a kid – he's only 15 – painted this of me today. He barely even glanced at me, and I was standing behind him when he made it."

Dan shook his head in disbelief. "How is that even possible?"

"Yeah, I agree. He's an autistic savant. He paints and draws for hours every day but hasn't spoken, ever. Not that anyone knows about, anyway."

"Huh! I'd never be able to pull that off," Dan said. "The speaking bit, I mean." He looked back at the painting. "Or this either, come to think of it."

Dulcie glanced over at her brother and laughed. He was such an extrovert. She couldn't imagine him *not* speaking. She closed the car door, carefully holding the painting away. "All right, back to work," she said.

"Yeah," Dan sighed. I've gotta go scrub down the boat. I hate that chore, but has to be done or it'll look terrible inside of a week." He gave his sister a wave and headed off in the direction of the waterfront.

Dan ran his own business, taking people on tours around Portland Harbor and Casco Bay in his small private yacht. Dulcie was his silent partner, and had invested an unexpected inheritance in his business to buy the boat. Dan lived on board and, with his natural storytelling abilities and ease with people, had made the business thrive.

Dulcie watched him walk away knowing that his momentary dejection would quickly pass. He loved everything about that boat. She clicked the lock on the door of the Jeep, noticing yet another scratch in the paint. Bringing the painting inside, she carefully set it on a table in her office, tipping it against the wall behind. She stood back and cocked her head sideways as she gazed at it. Xander Bellamy. She had heard of him, but it was the first time that she had met him.

Rachel knocked on the doorframe of Dulcie's office and walked in. She stopped immediately when she saw the painting. "That's awesome!" she said. "When'd you get that done? And why?" Her eyes grew big as she realized she'd just made a faux pas. "I mean, not 'why' exactly. But, it doesn't seem like something you'd do. Have a portrait made. Of yourself. Not that there's anything wrong with doing that," she was stammering now.

Dulcie turned and grinned at her assistant. "Easy, Rachel! No offence taken," she laughed. "I know what you're getting at. I'm not exactly the type for self-aggrandizement. I'd rather fade into the woodwork, given the choice." She looked over at the painting. "But this has kind of a weird story behind it. Have you heard of Xander Bellamy?"

Rachel thought for a moment. Her clear blue eyes squinted. "I know that name," she said slowly. Then she snapped her fingers. "He's the guy that was in the news a few months ago, right? Didn't his father kill his grandfather or something like that?"

Dulcie nodded. "Yes, and it was pretty sad. I just looked up the story. His mother had died several years ago, too. He's autistic and doesn't speak. His father was devoted to him but I guess the grandfather didn't have much to do with them, even though they all lived in the same house."

"Was he the father's father or the mother's? The grandfather, I mean," asked Rachel. She always tried to get the details straight, a trait that Dulcie loved since it helped with her work enormously.

"The mother's father."

"And didn't he fall off a balcony or out of a window or something like that?" asked Rachel.

"Yes, and there was some speculation that he was pushed by Xander although no one could imagine why. But then the father stepped forward and confessed that he had pushed him. They had been arguing, he said. It was all very strange and tragic."

"Sounds it," replied Rachel. "So how does Xander fit in with this?" she pointed to the painting.

"He did it," Dulcie said simply.

Rachel's eyes were wide. "*Really?*"

"Yup. And furthermore, he did it after barely looking at me, plus it only took him a few minutes. I've never seen anything like it. He started at the top, worked his way to the bottom, and never went back to change or touch-up anything. Just put down his brush and walked away when he was done."

"But how did he have the colors? Didn't he need to mix them?"

"He had a lot of paint on his palette already. The woman that takes care of him said that he's been doing a lot of portraits lately. I saw a whole bunch in his studio that looked like they were all of the same person. He just used the paint he already had to do my portrait."

"Did you ask him to? Why did he paint you?"

"I have no idea," said Dulcie. She hadn't thought about that. Why had he chosen to paint her? "Very good question. I have no idea," she repeated quietly.

"Well, that's a mystery for another time," said Rachel, adopting her businesslike voice. "Right now, we've got some logistics to figure out. You've got four more artists for the new exhibit with two or three works each, and then three more with single works, right?"

Dulcie took a deep breath and shifted gears mentally. "Yes," she nodded at the list Rachel was holding. "Could you do the usual with shipping and insurance and such? Do you have everyone's contact info?"

Rachel nodded, her curly hair bouncing. "No problem." She turned to Dulcie's portrait again. "Are you going to include this?" she asked. "That qualifies as Outsider Art, I'd think."

"It certainly does, but there is no way I'm putting a portrait of me in the gallery!" Dulcie saw Rachel trying to hide a smile. "So don't even think about it!" Dulcie added. "But I do plan on exhibiting some of his work. It's too incredible not to." She sat back in her chair. "The difficult part about this exhibit is that every piece has a different story about the artist that made it. I'll have to figure out a way to tell each story as briefly as possible."

"And tactfully, in some cases," Rachel added. "Anything else you need from me for now?" she asked.

Dulcie thought for a moment. "Nope. I think we're good for now, thanks."

Rachel was already heading for the door, her untamable hair bobbing up and down and her quick mind eager to take on the next project. Dulcie noticed she gave the bottle-cap-chewing-gum Statue of Liberty a wide berth.

CB

Adam Johnson wandered through the wine shop following his Portland Police Department partner and fellow detective, Nicholas Black, closely. Johnson tried to suck in his large stomach as much as possible and keep his arms pinned to his sides. He leaned over, ever so slightly, from time to time so that he could see an interesting looking label. A particular one caught his eye, and he gingerly picked it up. The label looked old, with ornate lettering.

"Pie-Not… pie-not NO-wer," he whispered to himself.

"Pinot Noir," Nick pronounced correctly over his shoulder.

"Pee-no newarr?" That sounds even worse!" Johnson said, aghast.

"It's a kind of grape," said Nick with a tinge of annoyance.

"Hmm," muttered Johnson, carefully replacing the bottle on the shelf. He shuffled behind Nick again as he moved to the next aisle.

Nick turned to face him. "Don't you have anything to do? You've been following me around for half the day now. I'm on lunch break, you know."

Johnson stared at the floor and stuffed his hands in his pockets. "Yeah, I know." He looked dejected.

Nick would have laughed but he knew his partner, Detective Adam Johnson, was serious. This really wasn't like him. "Hey," Nick said, "What's up?"

Johnson shook his head slowly, still looking down. "I'm in trouble," he said simply.

Now Nick was really concerned. Jovial, laid-back, devil-may-care Johnson was never in any trouble that he couldn't see himself out of within a very brief period of time. "Seriously? What sort of trouble?" Now that Nick thought about it, he hadn't even seen Johnson eating, which was a sure sign that something was wrong.

"It's this bet I have," Johnson began.

Nick's heart sank. Gambling? He would never have pegged Johnson as a gambler. Nick said quietly, "Do you need money, Adam?" Nick never called his partner by his first name, but the situation seemed so grave, he thought it was the right thing to say.

Johnson's head popped up again. "Well, now that you mention it…," he had a tiny twinkle in his eye, but it disappeared as he became lost in thought again.

"Okay, out with it!" Nick ordered.

Johnson sighed. "Fine. You'll find out soon enough. I've got a bet with the wife."

Nick relaxed with relief. At least it wasn't money. Or not serious money, at any rate. "And?" he said.

"And I'm losing."

"So what's the bet?"

Johnson shook his head with dismay again. "All right, here's the whole story. She made me go to the doctor for my snoring. She said it's like a freight train and she can't sleep. I bought her earplugs, but let's just say that that didn't go over well. So, I went to the doctor. He said I have sleep apnea. And high blood pressure. And I needed to lose weight. Otherwise, I'll have to wear some contraption when I sleep in case I don't breathe enough, and I'll have to go on some kind of blood pressure medication."

The gravity of the situation was beginning to dawn on Nick. Johnson really loved his food. "So you're on a diet?" he asked, trying not to smile.

"Yeah, you could say that. Plus, the wife and I made a bet. See, that was my big mistake. She said that I couldn't lose ten pounds in a month. She even gave me a back-up. I can either lose the ten pounds, or I can walk 300,000 steps. She gave me this," he took a little device off his belt. "It's a pedometer. She writes down how many steps I do every night." Johnson replaced it on his belt. "So far it's been a week. I haven't lost a pound, and I've only walked 37,562," he glanced at the device, "No, make that 63, steps."

Nick was laughing now. "Do I dare ask what happens if you lose?"

Johnson looked at the floor again and shoved his hands in his pockets. He said something that Nick couldn't hear.

"What's that?"

Johnson straightened up, eyed his partner squarely, and said, "A week for both of us at the La Dolce Vita Spa and Weight Loss Center. The former would be for her, the latter for me."

Nick began laughing harder. Johnson's wife was an adorable, petite Italian woman who commanded his life outside of his work. Johnson loved every second of it and everything about her. She was devoted to him as well. Nick had never known there to be any strife between them. "Is Maria upset with you?" he asked.

"No," Johnson said almost mournfully. "I think she's secretly hoping that I'll lose so she can go!"

Nick realized that, like Maria, he also assumed that Johnson would lose. Now he wondered what his end of the bet was. "What do you get if you win?"

Johnson instantly perked up. He stood straighter and a smile spread across his face like a ray of sunshine. "A week in Florida to see the Red Sox in spring training every day, including VIP tickets! And she gets me beer and sausages whenever I want them!" Johnson looked giddy. He rattled out the words so fast that Nick could barely understand them.

It was a grave situation, indeed.

A thought occurred to Johnson. "Hey! How 'bout if you wear this for a little while!" He started to take the pedometer off his belt again.

"Oh, no! No way! I'm not going to help you cheat!"

"Oh, c'mon! Just through lunch! I don't think it works right on me anyway. It doesn't count my steps right! Watch!" He walked down the aisle counting, then came back. "Ok, I said before I'd done something-something-63, right? So I just did fifteen steps It should be 78 now, right?" He looked down at the device, then back up at Nick. "Oh. It says 78. Okay, fine. It did work this time. But I swear…"

Nick shook his head and turned back to the wine selection. "Yeah, Johnson, I'd say you're in trouble. Right now, though, why don't you go outside and walk to the end of the block and back again. By the time you're at the door, I'll be done here. That should add maybe another hundred or so steps?"

Johnson sighed deeply and turned toward the door. "Yeah, okay. This place is kinda boring anyway."

*The job of the artist
is always to deepen
the mystery.*
~ Francis Bacon

CHAPTER TWO

Edith Bernstein was a decisive woman. She could size up anybody within the first ten seconds, and she was usually right. The only time that she had met Dr. Dulcinea Chambers, two years earlier, the conversation had consisted of exactly two words. "You'll do," she said.

"Congratulations," the board chairman had whispered to Dulcie after the woman had abruptly turned away. "Coming from her, that's a resounding endorsement. An unequivocal *'yes'.*" Dulcie was not encouraged. She was glad that Edith Bernstein's appearances in Maine were infrequent at best.

Truth be told, Dulcie was more than a little intimidated by the woman, but she was determined not to let it show. Edith Bernstein may have wealth and a certain lofty standing, but that was not why Dulcie needed to talk with her. The subject at the moment was Edith's nephew, Xander Bellamy.

Dulcie wanted to include his work in the new exhibit. She had even considered having Xander demonstrate his talents, but had quickly put an end to that idea. She didn't want him to seem like a circus side-show act. True, he did not speak and he lived a very closed and quiet life, but he seemed to project a level of dignity that Dulcie thought was too profound to be exploited. She had devised a possible solution, however. With Xander's father in prison though, Edith Bernstein was now Xander's guardian, and Dulcie needed her permission to carry out the idea.

They sat in what was most likely the "drawing room" of old days in the mansion that Edith now shared with Xander. Edith had just poured tea and handed Dulcie a cup. Dulcie had put it down quickly to avoid the nervous rattling. So far, Edith had said nothing. After pouring herself tea, which she drank absolutely black, she put down her cup and sat back in her chair.

"So," she asked sharply, "which have you come for? My money, or my approval?"

Dulcie took a very deep breath. "I think this would fit into the latter category," she said, forcing herself to look directly at Edith.

"Well, get on with it then," the woman said. "I'm not getting any younger."

Dulcie wasted no time. "I'm putting together an exhibit focusing on Outsider Art. It's a term that describes the artwork created by…"

"*Yes, yes*, I know what it is," Edith said waving her hand impatiently.

"Right," said Dulcie with a quick nod. "I was recently looking at your nephew's work, and I would like to include a few pieces of his in the exhibit."

"Fine," she said. The word shot out like a cannonball. "But that's not why you're here," she added.

"That's true," said Dulcie. "I'll get right to the point."

"That would be appreciated," Edith interjected.

"I would like to film Xander while he's painting, and show the video during the exhibit."

Edith paused. It was unusual for her. Dulcie held her breath. Edith considered the various aspects of the situation. Then, after a long five seconds, she said, "Yes. I'll need to see and approve of this video first, of course, before I can allow it to be shown. Now finish your tea." She pointed to Dulcie's cup.

Dulcie quickly lifted it and tried, unsuccessfully, not to slurp it down all it once. When she was finished she very carefully replaced the cup. "Of course, Mrs. Bernstein. I would be more than happy to share the video with you to make sure it's acceptable." Dulcie was trying to maintain her normal speaking tone, but her voice was rapidly emerging as a squeak. "Shall I coordinate with the housekeeper again to arrange a time to film Xander?"

"Yes," barked Edith. She saw Dulcie's cup was empty. "Thank you for coming by," she added more as a formality than a sentiment.

"Thank you, Mrs. Bernstein. I appreciate you taking your time to…"

"Yes, yes," said Edith, hoisting herself out of her chair. Dulcie quickly stood as well. Edith walked her to the door. As she was closing it behind Dulcie, she stopped. "I like you," she barked. "Don't screw it up." Then she shut the door firmly.

Dulcie barely made it back to her car before she began laughing.

☃

Giselle had dusted the upstairs and was proceeding to the first level of the house. She liked to work from the top to the bottom so that she could gauge the mood of the others as the day progressed. She had always risen early, not because she liked to, but because she had found it was the best way to avoid everyone. Of course now this wasn't entirely necessary, but it had become habit.

She had been with the family for nearly twenty years. Her life had been devoted to theirs. Perhaps she should have left a long time ago. But what would she have done? Where would she have gone? Besides, there was Xander to take care of. Her boy. She had fallen in love with him the moment his mother had brought him home. That was a good thing, since his mother had been completely incapable of helping him.

Xander's mother had died when Xander was seven years old. No one spoke of it. In actuality she hadn't died, she had killed herself. Not suddenly and decisively, but slowly and inevitably. Her life had been a constant battle with alcohol and sleeping pills, and she had finally succumbed. Giselle remembered how angry she felt that someone could throw away their own life like that, hurting the life of their child in the process. Especially this child. This child was special.

Giselle descended the stairs quietly and peeked in on Xander. He was painting, as always. Giselle opened the door a bit more, making it squeak. Xander did not acknowledge it or her in any way, yet she knew instinctively that he knew she was there.

"I'll make you some lunch in a little while, Xander. What about grilled cheese today? You haven't had that in a week or so, and I know you like it." He always gobbled down grilled cheese more quickly than the other lunches she made for him.

Xander continued to paint. He seemed unaware that she was speaking. Giselle stepped into the room to see what he was working on. She stopped quickly when she saw the canvas. It was that woman. The one from the museum. Giselle looked around and saw three other paintings of her leaning against the wall.

Xander had not painted a portrait of anyone but his father since he had been sent to prison two months earlier. Why this sudden change? Perhaps he was moving on with his thoughts? Did he actually have thoughts? Giselle simply shook her head and went back to the kitchen.

He had known she was there, of course. She was always there, always had been there. She was the one who helped him with everything. He never understood who she was, but she had always helped him. He knew that was good.

The other lady had not helped him very much. She had water coming from her eyes a lot. When the old man talked to her, shouted at her, her face bunched up and there was more water from her eyes. She always seemed to have a glass in her hand. She slept often. He had painted her sleeping several times. Then, one day, she didn't wake up and they took her away.

He was trying to understand the new lady that had visited, the one that he painted now. Painting helped him to understand people, in his own way. Most people were a mystery to him. They said and did things that never seemed to make any sense. For Xander, his life made complete sense. He got up every morning, washed, got dressed, ate, then he painted or drew. Sometimes he went for a walk with someone or they took him somewhere. Then he ate again. In the afternoon he painted and drew more, then he ate, then he went to bed.

When he wasn't doing these things, he was watching. He saw everything, every detail. Every nuance was cataloged in his mind. He could instantly recall any of the images, even those from years before when he was a little boy, and draw them with exact detail. It made him feel calm. Although he could never be able to describe it, drawing everything made him feel safe. It was how he put order into his world.

The noises many months before had made him feel unsafe. They had scared him. At night he often could hear shouting. Once he heard a scream and something breaking. He had covered his head with a pillow but he could still hear. He rocked back and forth that night, trying to be calm.

That's when he had begun the sketchbook. Something told him that he should not let anyone know. He made tiny, detailed sketches with a black pen. They did not record what he had seen like all the other drawings that he had made. Instead, they showed what he thought was happening around him. What things might look like. He kept the sketchbook hidden in his room.

They had lived in the big house with the old man for as long as Xander could remember. The old man and the other, younger one. Xander had seen that one, the younger one, holding the lady that had been taken away. He had seen water come from the man's eyes.

The old man had made Xander feel unsafe. Once the old man had taken one of Xander's paintings and thrown it hard into the fireplace where it burned. Xander did not know why he had done that. It was a perfect, detailed picture of the lady and the man. Xander had painted it several years after she had gone away. The one that burned showed them the way he had seen them once, with the corners of their mouths turned up.

Then, suddenly, the old man was gone. Xander thought that was good. The shouting had stopped. But then the younger man went away, too. Xander and the lady who made the food lived in the big house. That older lady had moved in, too. *Auntedith*. He kept hearing that sound. *Auntedith*. The older lady looked at him and shook her head a lot.

☙

Edith Bernstein slid her cardigan on over her crisp white cotton blouse. They were her wardrobe staples. When she had moved in to the mansion after her nephew-in-law had been sent to prison, she had brought exactly two suitcases. One contained her blouses, cardigans, straight skirts and slacks, and the other contained her shoes and her notebooks and files. That was all she needed.

Edith had no children of her own. She had married a much older man, who had promptly died and left her with quite a lot of money. Edith used it to travel the world extensively. She had few possessions because she wanted few possessions.

Her brother had been different. He was covetous and spiteful. He had also married money, a silly woman named Lily, much younger than himself, who had come with the added bonus of a child in tow. The little daughter was timid, meek, and pale. Her life with Oscar Bernstein didn't help. Oscar bullied her and the mother until one night, following a drunken spat, Lily had run off to the beach, tripped on some rocks, hit her head, then drowned in the incoming tide. It had been tragic.

Edith took her niece whenever she could, hoping to expand the girl's horizons. It had not worked. The girl was perpetually frightened by anything new. New York had been trying. London was a complete disaster. Eventually Edith gave up. How could she possibly put to right the lives of everyone else? Did they think she was a therapist or a magician? Or both?

One ray of hope had come in the form of Lawrence Bellamy who, inexplicably as far as Edith was concerned, fell in love with her niece. They married and moved to his home in Canada. Evidently finances were tight there, however, so they wound up living under Oscar's roof. With Xander's autism as a constant source of criticism from Oscar, his mother had inevitably unraveled.

Edith sighed. So much death in the family. Oscar had blamed Xander's mother for Xander's condition, saying it was her '*bad seed*' that brought shame on the family. She couldn't cope. No one knew if it was suicide or just an accidental overdose that had led to her early death. Not content to stop there, Edith's stupid brother now had to provoke his son-in-law on a continuing basis. Lawrence became the new target. Edith wouldn't have blamed him at all, even if he had actually done it. Oscar had it coming to him.

Edith just wished that her nephew had not made that confession. She knew exactly why he had. The police, inept as always, she thought with a snort, were beginning to think that Xander killed his grandfather by pushing him out the window. Edith had been outraged. Wouldn't it be so typical to take the easy way out and blame the 'crazy kid' who couldn't talk? Lawrence had stepped forward at that point and confessed. They questioned him again and again, but he kept to his story. Damned fool.

Edith looked in the mirror as she fastened the strand of pearls that were perpetually around her neck.

She could see a few more wrinkles at the corners of her eyes. Was it age, or just stress? She chose to believe it was the latter. She gave the pearls one last pat, turned from the mirror, and went down the hallway to see if she could persuade her nephew to go on a short walk.

Xander was in his studio, a large converted bedroom on the second floor of the mansion. It had huge, multi-paned windows that extended to built-in window seats below, letting the sunlight flood into the room. The windows looked over a stand of pine trees that cascaded down a steep hillside. Over the tops of the trees, the ocean extended in a vast, endless palette of blues and grays. Xander sat on one of the low seats in the window, drawing the birds flitting in the tops of the trees.

Edith stopped in the doorway and watched him for a moment. In her lifetime of travels, she had encountered many different kinds of people. She had learned to communicate at a basic level with nearly anyone, without the need for language. She was a straightforward, practical woman. Her communication, whether spoken or not, was the same.

Xander did not look up, but Edith knew that he had acknowledged her. He had stopped drawing just for a moment and looked briefly at the floor. He knew that she was there. She quietly walked up to him. She pointed to his shoes, then her shoes, then at the trees. He put down his sketchbook, stood, and followed her down the stairs and outside.

Edith saw Xander take a deep breath once they were outdoors. There was an onshore breeze, filled with the sweet smell of pine and sea spray. The closest expression to a smile that Xander ever made passed over his face. Edith knew that he was content. They continued slowly along the path that wound down through the trees and eventually opened onto a pebbled beach. The waves lapped against the little rocks softly.

Edith saw a nearby log and sat. She patted the space next to her, and he sat too. She sighed. "Xander, I'm not certain what to do next," she said aloud, knowing full well that he did not understand her. "Your grandfather is dead. That's fine, since he was a bullying bastard anyway. Your mother is dead. Your father is in prison." She shook her head fiercely. "He didn't do it. We all know that. He was stupid to confess."

Xander stared across the water. He heard her talking in her punctuated voice, but did not understand. He knew very few words. If any. He did understand what he saw, however. A whale had surfaced in the water. It was barely visible, its flat back disrupting the gentle waves only slightly, but his keen eye saw it. He watched it, keeping the picture etched in his mind with the millions of other images. For a brief moment, his mind pictured what the whale looked like under the water.

Expanding his images beyond what he saw, beyond simple recordings of the world around him, was something new. Sometimes he liked it. Now, picturing the whale under the water, he felt his body relax. He would not have known how to describe it, but anyone else would have said that they felt happy. Sometimes these images made him uncomfortable, however. His body tensed when they happened. Occasionally, his head ached. Those were the things that he drew in his sketchbook, hidden away. He put them there so that they would get out of his head.

With this Auntedith person, he relaxed. He did not understand that her dominant personality protected him, but somehow he felt it. He glanced over at her. She was still talking, her brow knitted into tight wrinkles. He would paint that when he got back.

"… so I guess I'm here for the duration," Edith continued, knowing she was talking to herself. "I've travelled so much, seen so much, I supposed it would be good for me to settle down for a while. I should probably go to the doctor and get a checkup. Haven't had one in years. Haven't seen the dentist either although these pearly whites seem to be holding up quite well." She clicked her teeth together as if to demonstrate. This made her think of food. Edith was a robust woman; she liked her food. "You must be getting hungry, Xander. Let's get back to the house and see what Giselle has in the kitchen." She rubbed her hand back and forth across his shoulders briefly, the most demonstrative sign of affection that she ever gave to anyone, and stood. He stood too and followed her back, looking over his shoulder one last time at the whale.

☙

Dulcie wasn't certain how to proceed. She wanted to hire a professional to video Xander, but did not want to overwhelm him, or anyone in the family, by showing up with a whole film crew. She knew that he certainly would not paint someone on cue. Besides, it would seem too much like a stunt if he did that. The whole point of this exhibit was to show how people's minds could work differently at the very core, creating in ways that others would not have normally considered.

"Maybe it's a stupid idea," she muttered aloud.

Rachel came in at that moment. "What's a stupid idea?" she asked sliding into the chair opposite Dulcie's desk.

Dulcie frowned. "This whole idea to video Xander Bellamy while he's painting someone's portrait. I'm just afraid it's going to look like a stunt. Or worse."

"Not if you do it right," said Rachel.

"What do you mean?"

"What if you treat it like a mini documentary? Maybe have a psychologist explain how they think Xander's mind works. I mean, it's pretty unbelievable what he can do." She glanced over at the portrait of Dulcie leaning against the wall.

Dulcie sat back in her chair and looked at the painting as well. "You know Rachel, that's actually not a bad idea," she said.

Rachel stood. "Yeah. That's why I get the big bucks!" she grinned. She was effectively moving up in the ranks at the museum, now that she was Dulcie's assistant.

Dulcie laughed. "Is that your way of asking for a raise?"

"Who, me?" Rachel said, tossing her curly hair, her eyes widening with mock innocence. "But for now, I have very important work to do. I'm going to run to the post office. Need anything?" She was already heading for the door.

Dulcie thought for a moment. "No, can't think of a thing. But thanks for asking. And for the great idea!"

"Anytime!" Rachel called out from the hallway.

The more Dulcie considered the idea, the more she liked it. She had been looking at the entire exhibit from the perspective of a museum curator. This was a different kind of exhibit, though. She had known that from the start. She needed to look at it from a psychologist's perspective.

The difficulty was, she wasn't a psychologist. She needed to find one who would work as a consultant. She rapidly did a search on her computer for local psychologists. The list was very long. "Ugh," she said. "This could take a while."

She thought of Xander again. Since he was quickly becoming the focus, perhaps she should start with him? He must have been diagnosed originally by someone. He may have had a doctor working with him at some point as well. It was worth a try.

Dulcie looked up a number and dialed.

"*Halooo?* Bellamy residence," the woman's voice said.

From the lightness of it, Dulcie knew the voice was Giselle's and not Edith's. "Hello, Giselle. This is Dulcie Chambers at the Maine Museum of Art. I have kind of an odd question. Do you know if a psychologist has ever worked with Xander? He must have been diagnosed originally by one," she paused.

"Yes," Giselle said. "Yes," she said again more softly. "There was one. I cannot think of the name. It was some time ago. Let me look through some things. Can I call you back?"

Dulcie could detect the traces of her French accent even through the telephone. French-Canadian, she decided. Quebec. She pushed the thought aside. "Yes, of course, Giselle. Let me give you my cell phone number," she replied.

Moments later, after she put down the phone, she thought, "*Bellamy. Hmmm. I think that's French. I wonder if the father was from Quebec?*" Not that it mattered, but Dulcie's mind couldn't help but attempt to solve a puzzle, even when it wasn't necessary.

Giselle slowly replaced the phone. She knew exactly who the doctor was. She knew how to reach him immediately. The trouble was, he also knew a few things about her. Facts that she preferred to keep secret. Perhaps he would not say anything. After all, wasn't there doctor-patient confidentiality? Yet, she had not been his patient. She had been his lover. And as such, she had confided in him far too much.

It was his way. Somehow he was able to manipulate conversations so that people would talk, open up, confide. He asked the right questions, but they never seemed overly personal. Yet, before long, one found oneself telling him things that had not even been told to the closest of friends.

Giselle did know one thing about him that could work to her advantage, however. It was his Achilles' Heel. Dr. Raymond Armand was a very ambitious man. He had already gained some notoriety within the New England medical community for working with autistic patients. Giselle knew that he would not turn down an opportunity to promote himself.

She quickly looked up his number and dialed. The phone rang several times. She was considering if she would actually leave a message for him or just hang up, when he answered.

"Ah, Dr. Armand! We have not spoken in quite some time. It is Giselle," she said quickly, her slight French accent becoming more pronounced through nervousness.

Silence on the other end. Had he forgotten who she was?

"Giselle!" she could tell he was smiling. "It has been too long! And how are you?"

"I am quite well, thank you. But I have not called socially, I am sad to say." She wasn't sad at all, of course. She wanted to get to the point quickly. "I am calling on behalf of another. The director of the art museum in Portland. She wishes to speak with you."

"Well, certainly," he replied, somewhat confused. He knew of Dr. Chambers, of course. She had an excellent status within the community. Then he sighed. She probably wanted to talk with him about a donation. If that was the case, however, why would Giselle be calling?

"It is somewhat delicate," Giselle continued. "You see, it concerns Xander. The museum is exhibiting some of his work. I know that you cannot reveal the medical *confidences*," she pronounced the word in the French way, "but I think she wishes to know about his condition generally."

"Well certainly, I can be of assistance," he replied. He was still unclear as to why Giselle was calling instead of Dr. Chambers.

"Good, good. But speaking of *confidences*, I would like to keep any that are between us private? Although I know the Bellamy family well, I do not believe that any personal information that I shared with you should be known. I, in turn, would not share any personal *confidences* of yours, either."

Raymond Armand thought for a moment. He had not recalled sharing any personal confidences with her during any of their interludes. In fact, he never shared his personal confidences with anyone. He chose to remain silent regarding this small fact for the moment however. Nothing could be gained by it at present.

"Of course, Giselle. This is a professional matter, and will certainly remain so," he said.

Giselle sighed in relief. "I thank you, *Raymond*. I will contact this Dr. Chambers and provide your telephone number. I believe she will be calling you shortly," Giselle concluded in a businesslike voice.

Raymond nearly laughed at her obvious attempt at curtness. "I'll look forward to it. It's very good to hear from you again, Giselle," he added softly.

"Yes, that is nice. Good bye, *doctor*," she said.

She put down the phone with a hand that was shaking slightly and began dusting a bookshelf that was so spotless, she could see her uneasy reflection.

CHAPTER THREE

Dr. Raymond Armand stood in Dulcie's office looking at the portrait of the woman standing beside him. "It is astonishing what he can do," he said at last. He leaned forward, holding up his wire-rimmed reading glasses and peering through them to see detail.

Dulcie eyed him thoughtfully while he examined the painting. *"Quite good looking,"* she thought. Thick dark hair, dark eyes, a somewhat brooding Mediterranean appearance. He was wearing a white linen shirt with the collar open under a light tweed sport jacket. In spite of herself, Dulcie thought she might possibly be attracted to him, although he wasn't exactly what would be considered *her type*. Still…

He stepped back beside her, jarring her from her less-than-professional meditations. Her cheeks reddened slightly. *"Dulcie stop it! He's just a psychologist, not a mind reader,"* she thought.

Raymond had, in fact, read her mind in this case. He was quite used to the reaction. He knew that he exuded a certain sex-appeal, and used it to his full advantage.

"What was your first reaction?" he asked.

Dulcie nearly stammered thinking that he was referring to her thoughts on himself. She realized quickly that he meant her reaction toward Xander. "That's an interesting question," she said to cover her momentary confusion. "Actually, my first reaction was that he appeared to be very thoughtful," she said.

Raymond nodded. "He is. Of course, as my patient, there are certain things that I cannot share with you, but I can tell you that although he does not speak, he certainly understands the world around him. In his own way."

"In his own way," Dulcie repeated. "That's what confuses me. What way is that?" she asked.

"He is what we believe to be a visual processor. His mind works almost entirely on visual knowledge. Verbal communication, which all of us in the hearing world understand very well and have since birth practically, he does not process. And it is not simply a matter of speech. If you were to attempt to teach him sign language, reading, any sort of advanced communication, you would fail utterly. Our language, any language, is actually a code. His brain does not process code. He can, however, connect specific images with specific actions. It's probably quite similar to the way some animals or birds process the world around them," Raymond explained.

"Animals?" Dulcie said, surprised. "That sounds like he doesn't have as much intelligence."

"That's how many see it, but how do we define intelligence, exactly? Animals and birds have a great deal more understanding than we do regarding many things. We just believe that we're superior, but are we really?"

"Good point," Dulcie said. She was silent for a moment. "I wish we could know how he thinks."

"I do to. But we can get a glimpse of it in his artwork. He sees everything, and that is what makes him wonderful. He sees what no one else can."

Dulcie was mesmerized by the doctor's speech. She simply stared at the portrait of herself. She had looked at it before, several times, but now she really *looked* at it. She saw a woman who looked confused. How had he been able to capture that? How had she missed it? Now she wanted to see more of his work.

"Dr. Armand," she began.

"Oh please, please… *Raymond*," he insisted.

The casual request seemed more like an intimacy. She felt self-conscious. "Raymond," she began again, trying to sound as businesslike as possible, "I know something about the tragedy in Xander's household. It was in the news so it would be hard not to know about it. Do you think that has affected him?"

"Most certainly. People that he has lived with for quite some time are now missing. I don't know if he completely understands life and death. For that matter, I can't say that I completely understand life and death," he added somewhat self-deprecatingly, "but his surroundings, his companions, have changed quite suddenly. That has to affect him in some way."

"I was told that he painted his father over and over again after he was sent to prison," Dulcie said. She turned quickly to face Raymond. "Do you really think he did it? Do you really think Lawrence Bellamy pushed his father-in-law through the window?"

Raymond Armand chuckled. This is why the tabloid press would always have a place in society. People needed to talk about these things – the tragedies in other's lives. "In my professional opinion, he does not fit the profile. To push someone out of a window would either be a premeditated act, or an impulsive act of rage. I have met Lawrence Bellamy on several occasions and he is neither a man who plans things out, nor is he impulsive. What I did see was a man who is soft. Perhaps *gentle* is a better word. He wants nothing more than to shut out the world and protect his son."

"Then you must have known that his confession was wrong!" Dulcie exclaimed.

"Of course I did. Nearly everyone did. But he was so convincing that the court had no alternative but to believe him," Raymond said. "I'm sure that was why he received such a light sentence for what would ordinarily be a heinous crime."

"He thought that Xander did it," Dulcie said quietly. "Didn't he."

"I'm sure he did. Why else would he have left the one person that he wanted to protect? It was the only way that he could protect him, in that case."

"It can't be true," Dulcie said. "Xander couldn't have done it himself. That doesn't make any sense either. It must have been someone else," she said. "But I remember reading that his father was the only one in the house at the time. Xander and the housekeeper were out on the grounds, although there was speculation that Xander could have gone back into the house…" Dulcie trailed off.

Raymond did not like the direction that the conversation was taking. He artfully switched focus. "For now it is best to consider Xander. I believe you brought me here to discuss a project that you're working on? Showing a video of Xander at work during the exhibit? I must say it sounds very interesting!" He used his smoothest voice, calculated to flatter, and distract, Dulcie.

It worked. Her thoughts turned to her work. "Yes, but here's the tricky part. I don't want him to look like some sort of oddity. That's where you come in. I'd like to have you as part of the project, to narrate and explain who Xander is and how his mind works."

Raymond nodded, outwardly serious, but inwardly pleased. This was perfect! He loved the idea of being the expert for this project, especially if his work was on public display. Everyone would see him and hear his words directly. Several would be very wealthy and influential museum patrons, influential in directions beyond art. This could be the step forward that his career desperately needed right now. He took a deep, silent breath to steady his voice. "I'd be honored to help. What's your next step?"

"My next step is to look at Xander's work again, and to watch him work. Before I hire expensive videographers, I want to know exactly what they should be showing."

"Very good. Why don't I join you while you're with Xander and I can offer some insights."

"Perfect," Dulcie said happily. She felt relieved that the project was at last coming together. "I'll make the arrangements and get in touch. Thanks so much for your assistance, Doct..., um, I mean, Raymond." She stuck out her hand somewhat awkwardly to shake his.

He gently put out his hand and held hers for a moment. "The pleasure is mine," he said.

ᚳ

Dan Chambers had scrubbed the decks and benches of the boat until they glistened. He always abhorred the task before he began, but by the time he was done, he was happy. It seemed to cleanse his thoughts, performing the mindless scrubbing.

His thoughts didn't necessarily need cleansing; they were never of the horrific sort. But he did find himself thinking about too many things at once. His brain seemed to like tangents. He was lost in one as he tossed the scrub brush back into the bucket of sudsy water, and did not notice the man that had slowly walked up the dock and stopped beside the yacht.

"Looks good," he said, jarring Dan from his thoughts. Dan jerked his head up quickly. He was looking directly at Detective Nicholas Black.

"Thanks," Dan said, without enthusiasm. He wiped off his hands with a towel. "What can I do for you," he added in a curt, businesslike voice.

Nick sighed and looked away. He had expected that. He and Dan had started off well, but Nick's situation with Dulcie had quickly changed everything. He should have been honest with her. He should have told her everything. He hadn't pursued her, but his developing feelings had become apparent, to the point where he knew she was interested too.

Dan was simply being protective of his sister, and Nick knew that he had to earn back his trust, along with Dulcie's. "Looks like you're done here. Do you have a minute? Could I talk with you?" Nick desperately wanted to clear the air.

Dan's initial glare gradually changed to a resigned look. He jerked his head toward the yacht's cabin. "C'mon in," he said. "We might as well sit down and we can't here," he motioned toward the wet bench beside him. "It'll take a while for all this to dry."

Scuffing off as much dirt from his shoes on the dock as he could, Nick stepped on board. He followed Dan into the sunny cabin. Dan gestured toward a bench by a table and opened the refrigerator. "Suppose you wouldn't turn down a beer," he said without looking up. "And don't tell me you're on duty."

"I'm not and I wouldn't," Nick said. He took the bottle and screwed off the cap.

"So," Dan said sitting opposite him. He was expressionless. Unlike his sister, he was an excellent poker player. "What can I do for you?" he repeated.

Nick took a long drink. "First of all, I'm sorry. I should have told you, and Dulcie, all about my situation. I didn't and it was stupid."

"Yeah it was," interjected Dan quietly.

"I've already apologized to Dulcie, but I wanted to apologize to you, too." He swirled the beer around and looked down into the bottle as though all of the answers were hidden inside. "I like Dulcie a lot," he said quietly.

Dan understood Nick's dilemma. He wanted to relent and tell the guy that he would put in a good word, but his loyalty to his sister was steadfast. "Look," he said. "I can't go to bat for you. Dulcie is pretty strong-willed, as you may have noticed, and you broke her trust. Mine too, for that matter, but I think I can probably forgive you a lot sooner than she can. You're gonna have to handle this one on your own. But I can tell you that I won't say anything negative about you. I know you got yourself into a pretty rotten situation and probably no one handles things like that perfectly. So I'll give you the benefit of the doubt. But that's about as far as I can go at this point."

Nick was surprised by the long speech. He nodded. "That's all I'm asking for. I appreciate it." He gazed out the window for a few moments. The wind was getting stronger, making dark rippled patches across the water's surface. "How is she?" he asked.

"Busy, as always," Dan replied. "She's got some new project called outside art...no, that's not it.

Outsider art. Not art outdoors, but people who aren't actually artists. Well they are, but they're not. OK, she can explain it a lot better."

"I think I get the picture," said Nick, taking another long drink.

Dan was a talker. He couldn't help it. His mind was on a new subject and with Nick a willing listener, Dan had to keep going until he had exhausted the topic. Or until Nick looked bored. That was usually what happened first. Fortunately for him, Dan had learned at a young age to notice the signs of a listener getting bored.

"She's got this thing in her office right now. It's the Statue of Liberty, made by some homeless guy out of bottle caps and gum! Like, chewing gum! It's as tall as I am! Kind of gross, but still, a lot of work."

"Now *that* I have to see," said Nick.

"Yeah, she also just showed me a portrait that some kid had done of her. He saw her for about a minute, then painted this amazing portrait, incredibly accurate, with her standing behind him. She couldn't believe it." Dan stopped and looked over at Nick. "Hey, you might know about him. He's that kid whose dad went to prison for pushing the kid's grandfather out of a window."

The Bernstein case. Nick hadn't worked on it, but he knew all about it. He wished that he had been assigned to it, because he had never liked the outcome. The confession of Lawrence Bellamy never made any sense to him, but the man had insisted he had done it.

"Xander Bellamy?" Nick asked, trying to look less interested than he was.

Dan nodded, swallowing the last of his beer. "Yup, that's the name. Dulcie's going to put some of his work in the exhibit, but not the one of her. I think she should, but she'd never do that. She hates attention."

Nick had known that. Dulcie had told him as much. She didn't like the social gatherings and their inherent fundraising that were such an integral part of her job. They put the spotlight squarely on her, and that was contrary to her nature. Nick had attended far too many of those gatherings in his former life, which was yet another reason why he had left it all behind. His ex-wife, he still shuddered thinking of her, had loved them.

Nick finished his own drink, stood up, and put the bottle by the sink. "Thanks," he said nodding toward the empty bottle. "And thanks for being honest. I'll do my best to put things right," he said.

Dan stuck out his hand, and Nick shook it quickly. "Like I said," Dan repeated, "You didn't exactly handle the situation well, but I won't stand in your way. I'll warn you though, you've got a lot of work to do."

Nick simply grimaced, nodded, and made his way back up onto the dock.

The September wind had been threatening a chill in the air. The days were warm, but the wind was an omen. Winter was coming. Nick had a love-hate relationship with winter. He loved the longer nights. He would reserve thick books, or entire series, for the winter when he could settle in for an evening. All year he fortified his wine collection so that in the winter, he could simply come home, open a bottle of something good, make dinner, and let himself become lost in a good story.

Yet, his job didn't stop in the winter. With less daylight, he often had to cram in as much as possible if he was working on a case. And he was nearly always working on a case. He had risen to the status of detective quickly after joining the Portland Police force as an officer. Originally the job had been an escape, taking him away from his seemingly predestined life. His family was Boston Brahmin on both sides, and it had been the expectation from the start that he would marry the person that they chose and become a lawyer to continue the family legacy in the firm that his grandfather had founded.

In the end, Nick could do neither. He did not rebel; he simply walked away. His parents would not forgive him. He hadn't spoken with them in several years. Nick had made ends meet living in a tiny studio apartment above a bar in Portland.

Although he liked to believe that he didn't need it, Nick had at last received a tidy inheritance from his grandparents. Within the past month it had allowed him to move out of the studio and into one of the condos that perched out on the wharf overlooking the harbor. He also bought a new car, just in time as it turned out since the previous rust-bucket had been breaking down throughout the summer. Nick told himself that the money would not change his life. It simply made him a bit more comfortable.

It certainly didn't change his work ethic. He had found his calling. Somehow, it was in his blood. Nick had a strong sense of right and wrong; he believed in rules and treating others fairly, with kindness and dignity, wherever it was warranted. His work made him privy to the depths of many peoples' characters. He had seen how selfish and mean people could be. He had also seen how desperate.

Nick walked along Commercial Street toward his home thinking about the Bernstein case. Lawrence Bellamy had confessed out of desperation. Nick knew that. Although it hadn't been assigned to him, Nick couldn't help but read all of the reports as they came in. The whole thing was unsettling. Something about it wasn't right.

The man who had been killed, Oscar Bernstein, was by all accounts a difficult man. He had outlived his wife by many years. His step-daughter was once considered quite beautiful, but toward the end of her short life was referred to as "sickly." Nick realized that the sickness was most likely alcoholism. She had married Lawrence Bellamy, and their son was Xander.

According to the reports that Nick remembered, Oscar had never been pleasant toward any of them. He allowed his step-daughter's family to live at his mansion but otherwise was never kind. Quite the reverse, in fact. Nick could only imagine the daily turmoil within the household.

For that reason, perhaps Xander's condition was in some ways a blessing. He couldn't know of the unhappiness surrounding him. Then Nick considered what he himself knew about autism, which was very little. He slowed his pace. Perhaps Xander did know of the unhappiness. Perhaps he knew far more than anyone realized.

There was little Nick could do about any of it now, however. The case was closed. Still, he could see if it was possible to wheedle an invitation to the art museum's opening of the new exhibit. If Xander's work was being shown, it might give Nick some insights. Not that any reason other than interest in the Oscar Bernstein case would compel him to attend....

‿

Dr. Raymond Armand sat at the desk of his stylishly sparse office peering through his reading glasses at his computer screen. He needed the glasses only slightly, but he liked to use them more than necessary as he felt they gave him a certain air of intellectualism. He had decorated his office in shades of ivory and pewter gray, complimented by stainless steel and glass. He felt it was tranquil. Others, the ones who didn't come back, referred to it as industrial. Not in a good way.

Throughout the previous decade he had worked very hard to carefully cultivate his aura. Originally born *Raymond Armand Brown* he had dropped the surname after receiving his doctorate and always used the full name of "Raymond." Somehow, 'Ray Brown' did not fit the image that he wanted to convey. Technically, he could use the title of *doctor* although it was not of the medical type. His degree was in psychology, not psychiatry. He had never attended medical school. His alma mater was a tiny college in northern California that happened to award doctorates in a small number of subjects with comparatively low graduation requirements. He had certainly earned his PhD., yet it was not of the lofty status that he would have others believe. It wasn't a lie, even if it wasn't entirely the truth. He was comfortable charging high rates for his time because he believed that his time was worth a great deal of money. Whether or not this was actually the case was beside the point. When one sets a high price and believes in it, others begin to believe it, too. It was a beautiful cycle of self-justification.

Raymond had chosen to move to Portland for its size and proximity to Boston. In Portland he would have far less competition than he would have in other more major cities. Yet being near Boston, he could attend conferences and social events easily that would elevate his status. So far, it had worked. He had been able to align himself with a few research projects from more prominent universities and had his name on several publications, albeit further down on the author lists.

After ten years, however, he had yet to be the primary name on any published professional papers. This fact had irked him for some time. He had never encountered a patient with suitable concerns that could warrant any kind of case study. Xander Bellamy had been the closest he had come.

When Xander's father had sought his counsel regarding Xander, Raymond had at first been skeptical. What use could a shut-away boy with autism be to his own career? Perusing the recent research on the condition, however, Raymond quickly realized that it was the latest hot topic in the world of psychology and indeed amongst the general public. The popularity would make it that much easier for him to get a written case study published. The selfish fact that he would be using Xander to advance his own career never crossed his mind. The additional fact that he probably would not be helping Xander in the least, or anyone else like him, was of no concern to Raymond.

Everything had gone quite well until he made the mistake of discussing his intentions to use Xander as a case study with Oscar Bernstein. Xander's father knew of Raymond's plan and did not disapprove. Oscar, however, would not allow it. And since Oscar paid the bills, Oscar was in charge. Raymond had been promptly dismissed.

After Oscar was killed, and suspicion had implicated Xander, Raymond had given psychological testimony in court regarding Xander's condition. It had quickly been established that the boy was incapable of standing trial. Raymond had suggested that Xander be placed in a facility for the mentally ill. That was when Xander's father, Lawrence Bellamy, had confessed.

Raymond sat back from the computer and took off his glasses, twirling them around in his hand absentmindedly. This art museum project could certainly prove interesting. Not only did it involve Xander, the autistic savant, but it had the advantage of the family being in the news during the murder trial. Built-in publicity, even if it was of the scandalous sort. Raymond simply could pick up where he left off with his case study, this time with the added bonus of notoriety. He had to make the most of it.

Making the most of it could certainly include a bit of personal enjoyment, he thought as he remembered his meeting with Dulcie Chambers. She was decidedly attractive and, if he was not mistaken, which he never was, she had found him so as well. He smiled. Yes, that could be an enjoyable side benefit. "In fact," he said aloud, "why not start now?"

He looked up her number and was about to dial, then thought better of it. A trip to the museum would be much more effective. True, he did run the risk of her not being there, but if she was, he could catch her off guard. He put on his jacket then pulled a mirror from his desk drawer to check his hair. Perfect, as always.

Moments later he sauntered down the street feeling quite confident. She had, after all, requested his services. This could be most beneficial in so many ways.

As he approached the museum, he was briefly caught off guard as Dulcie stepped out of the front door.

"Dr. Armand! Oh, sorry, I mean *Raymond* of course," she smiled at him.

"Yes, it's always just *Raymond* for you, please!" he said with a self-deprecating gesture. "I was just coming in to speak with you, but I see you're off somewhere important."

"Yes, very important," Dulcie replied. "I'm going to get a cappuccino around the corner. Would you like to join me? We can talk there."

"Absolutely," he said. As they turned, he touched the small of her back, leading her forward.

"*Hmmm. A tad intimate*," thought Dulcie. But then again, as a psychologist, perhaps it was just his nature to make people feel more connected and calm? "So tell me what brings you down to see me," Dulcie asked aloud.

"I've been thinking about Xander, of course," Raymond said. "After we discussed him in your office, I began remembering certain specifics. For example, after examining him, watching his behavior, I quickly realized that he only draws or paints what he sees. It is never from his imagination."

"Are you saying that he has no imagination? That would mean that he isn't creative, that he only records his surroundings."

"Ah, that's an interesting extension of the concept. And I suppose that you're concerned that he is not a true artist if he is not creative."

"It is something to consider," she said. They had reached the café and he held the door for her. Dulcie was feeling as though he was being a bit too presumptuous so she quickly marched toward the counter and ordered her coffee. Then she turned to him and said, "This is my treat. I insist since you're providing all of this insight. What would you like?"

"*Very good!*" he thought. "*She is not easily manipulated. And she reads people well. I'll have to be more subtle with her.*" He glanced briefly at the menu of drinks on the wall and ordered a latte.

They turned to the nearest table and sat as the barista began making the espresso machine hiss. Dulcie took off her jacket and draped it on the chair beside her. "So, he may not be creative. He may simply be kind of a human photographer."

Armand chuckled. "That's one way of putting it. But consider this, Dulcie. Are all photographs simply a record? Are none creative? Many photographs are considered art because the photographer sees what we cannot. Isn't this true?"

Why hadn't Dulcie thought of that? She was annoyed with herself. Given half a second more, she would have. He was unnerving. She didn't like the feeling.

"Very true, but is this what Xander is doing? Does he see what we don't? Does he see the world differently?"

"What do you think?" Armand asked. He smiled winningly at the young woman now placing their steaming cups on the table. "*Molto bene*," he murmured in Italian. "*Grazie*."

Dulcie looked away and firmly held her mouth closed. She did not want to acknowledge his attempt at sounding urbane. She sipped her cappuccino tentatively to mask her annoyance. "What do I think?" she said aloud at last and paused. "What I think, is that I need to see Xander, and his work, a great deal more before I can pass judgment."

Armand was instantly concerned. "Does this mean you may not include him in the exhibit?" His plan to promote himself could be unraveling. He had to convince her that it was still a good idea.

"I'm not certain," said Dulcie, sensing his concern but not sure of why it was apparent. Perhaps he didn't want to lose the project? It would certainly enable him to charge a relatively hefty consultation fee. She decided to string him along. "Xander has a talent, obviously, and it does fall under the heading of *art brut*." She did not bother to define this for him. "*If he's so witty with languages, he can figure it out*," she thought.

Raymond had no idea what *art brut* was. He realized, however, that to succeed with Dulcie he would have to change tactics. She did not respond to borderline patronization. He decided to try a more straightforward approach. "I'm afraid I don't know that term. What does it mean?" he asked looking at her directly.

Now Dulcie was momentarily unnerved. She hadn't expected him to admit any sort of weakness. Perhaps he had decided to remove the façade? Good. She preferred the direct approach. "It's also known as *Outsider Art*. It's a term that refers to works of art made by people that we would not consider to be professional artists. They are compelled to create simply for the process. Tramp art falls under the category, as well as art compulsively created by those who are insane."

"Would you consider autism a kind of insanity?" Armand asked.

This question was extremely disconcerting. "Well…" she considered for a moment. "It would depend on how you define insanity."

"Very true. To the layman, insanity provokes fear. To the lawyer, insanity implies lack of culpability. The term has come to mean so many things that in the psychiatric professions, it is not even used. Instead, we simply refer to these conditions as mental disorders."

Dulcie was thoughtful as she looked down into her nearly empty cup. "You're right about provoking fear. I hadn't thought about that, but it does."

"Are you fearful of Xander?" Armand asked.

Dulcie shook her head instantly, swallowing the list sip of cappuccino. "Not at all. He seems so gentle. Tell me," she put down her cup now that it was empty. "How much were you able to do with him? I mean, did you spend quite a bit of time with him?"

Armand paused. How much should he tell her? Would it be prudent to divulge everything? Probably not. "I initially evaluated him. Then I provided expert opinion after the unfortunate death of his grandfather," he said.

"I see," she nodded. Glancing at her watch she added, "I'm so sorry, but I have to get going. I have yet another meeting," she said with a slight frown. "It seems my days are filled with them now." He hadn't finished with his coffee, but started to get up anyway. "No, no!" Dulcie exclaimed. "Don't rush just for me. Finish and enjoy. Thanks so much for the conversation." She hurriedly rattled her cup on its saucer over to the counter, grabbed her coat, and with a small wave to him, pushed through the door.

Dulcie had not seen Detective Nicholas Black standing outside. She was heading quickly in the opposite direction. She had not seen him walk by the window several minutes before, stop immediately, then attempt to peer inside without looking obvious. As he watched her chatting with Dr. Raymond Armand, Nick's heart had lurched, pounding against his chest.

Dulcie had not seen him, but from the corner of his eye, Raymond had. And although they had never met, Raymond knew exactly what Nick was thinking.

CHAPTER FOUR

No one appreciated order more than Edith Bernstein. Where she found any sort of disorganization, she would apply her wealth of skills and patience to make the chaos conform to one of her myriad of systems. No one was exempt. This included her nephew, Xander.

Edith realized that she had to show some restraint in this particular case, however. Xander had his own order, his own systems, for organizing his world. He rigidly followed these systems. Edith was careful to observe him and quickly learned where and how they applied. Where there was no system, however, Edith felt that she had free reign. She had awakened to a rainy day, which was perfect for tackling the paintings in Xander's studio.

Dressed as always in a cardigan and sensible shoes, Edith firmly stepped into the studio and headed straight for the paintings in the corner. The walls were lined with canvases, as many as ten deep. They overlapped each other so that Edith couldn't get a rough estimate of how many there were. She started counting, touching each lightly with her finger and whispering each number.

Xander worked quietly, as he always did, on his latest painting. While Edith was counting, however, his head began to bob up and down with the rhythm. His lips moved slightly. He stopped painting and kept moving with the rhythm.

Sensing something different in the room, Edith stopped and turned around. Xander continued to bob up and down while his lips continued to move. After several seconds, he stopped. Without acknowledging Edith, or anything else, he started painting again.

Edith was intrigued. She had never seen him interact. At one point, when he was quite young, he had used basic hand signals, but since his father had been sent away, since the shocking death of his grandfather, he had not acknowledged the outside world in any way that Edith knew of. She started counting again, then stopped quickly. He bobbed and moved his lips, as he had before, then stopped abruptly and changed colors on his brush.

Edith turned back to her work. She was a practical woman and did not feel that a situation required pondering. It was either obvious or it wasn't. Xander had just interacted with her albeit in a rudimentary way. She knew he had done this in the past. Why not do it again, she reasoned. That was all she needed to know about the situation.

She began moving the paintings along the wall to create stacks. She had decided to classify them by subject. Older ones were of Xander's mother. Edith found several of Giselle. Only two were of Xander's grandfather. Many, especially more recent ones that still smelled of paint, were of his father. Edith picked these up gingerly in case they were still wet. She didn't care whether the painting was harmed, but she didn't want to get paint on her cardigan. It was worn and old, but certainly not in need of replacement yet. No need to rush things, especially when it came to spending unnecessarily.

She steadily worked her way into the mass of artworks. Putting down yet another of Xander's father, she began to step away when something caught her eye. She stooped over and looked more closely.

The painting showed Xander's father in what had been Oscar Bernstein's study. Edith could make out his desk in the background, and the windows were obviously the same. Her nephew-in-law had a look of despair on his face. Xander was extremely good at capturing emotions, which Edith found odd given his condition. What had caught her eye, however, was a small figure in the background. Edith squinted and groped at her chest for her reading glasses, hanging by a cord around her neck. She flipped them open firmly and placed them squarely on her nose. Then she leaned closer.

She was staring into the tiny face of her brother, Oscar Bernstein. He was laughing, his features contorted into a nearly maniacal form that she had, unfortunately, had the great displeasure of having seen far too many times in her youth. It was the look that he had when he was laughing at someone, usually when he had just exerted his narcissistic ego successfully. The old feelings of disgust washed over her as she looked at his painted image. He wore his "evening robe" as he liked to call it, a royal blue silk wrap. His green-pajamed legs and slippers stuck out beneath it. He was standing beside his desk. The window behind him was the one that he had fallen through on the evening of his death. It was open.

Edith knew that the pajamas and robe were the clothes he had worn when he died. And as she looked more closely at the painting, she could make out a shadow. It was the shadow of another person in the room. Someone other than her nephew. Someone that Lawrence would not have even seen.

Edith knew that Xander only painted what he saw. The psychologist had told her that. All of Xander's paintings showed evidence of that. Had he really been there that evening? In Lawrence's confession, he had insisted that he was the only other person in the house, that he and his father-in-law had argued, and that he had become so angry, he pushed him out of the window. No one could find evidence of the death not occurring in this manner. The judge was forced to believe the story.

It would have been unusual for Xander to be out at that time, but it had been a summer evening and the sun was just setting. Giselle said that she had taken Xander for a walk down the path to the ocean, since it had been so hot during the afternoon. She liked to get him outdoors at least once each day. Yet it was possible that they had come back in time for him to look into his grandfather's study. He passed by it on the way to his studio. It was possible....

Edith stepped back from the canvas and took off her glasses. She glanced over at Xander. He was working away, as usual, his face blocked by the easel in front of him. Not that it mattered. He wouldn't take notice of anything that Edith looked at, she was sure. She picked up the painting and set it to one side. Quickly she sorted through the remainder of the canvases. She hoped to find another similar to this odd one, but had no luck.

Would Xander notice if she took this painting from the room? Would he notice of she moved it into her room? With her most abrupt, businesslike manner, she picked it up, moved so that he could not see the front of it, and strode from the room.

Xander had not even looked up, yet he knew exactly what had happened. He knew which painting she had taken. He knew that one was different. Different from the others. He had felt different making it. He knew that she would be interested in it. Even though he had no real understanding of the concept, he somehow knew that it told a story.

Edith brought the painting in to her bedroom and closed the door behind her. She put it on the bed, dragged a chair close to the window, then propped the painting on it so that she could see it in the light better. Although it was a dark day, she could make out more detail than she had seen in the corner of Xander's studio.

Oscar Bernstein was, most certainly, laughing. She had hated that laugh. There was nothing in the painting to indicate why he would be laughing. The figure was so small in the background, it was difficult to tell the direction that he was looking. He seemed to be leaning backwards, his head tilted back slightly as he laughed. The window was probably about three steps behind him. Would someone in the room have been angry enough to lunge forward and push him out the window? Perhaps Lawrence could have turned back around quickly and charged toward Oscar. Perhaps the other person in the room could have waited for Lawrence to leave, then stepped forward to launch Oscar out of the window. Perhaps Lawrence and the other person could have been working together.

Edith sat down on the edge of the bed. She did not like mysteries. Her mind was in constant motion attempting to remove complication, not to find it.

She thought about Lawrence and sighed. He had never stood a chance against his father-in-law. He was a good husband for his timid wife, Gisa, and without the difficulties from Oscar Bernstein or a son with a condition such as Xander's, might have been able to keep Gisa from sinking into her state of depression and alcoholism. With the combined burdens, however, it was too much to ask of Lawrence Bellamy. He had to make a choice, and he chose to focus on his son. Edith reflected on the notion for a moment. Without children of her own she did not have any means for comparison, yet the more she considered Lawrence's options along with his capabilities, she knew that she would have made the same decision. He had essentially sacrificed his wife for his son. He could not have helped both. He only had the power and stamina to choose one.

Edith stood and went to the window. She blamed herself for some of the tragedy. She knew Oscar's character. When he had demanded that Lawrence's family move in to the mansion or not receive a penny of his considerable money, it was for his own selfish benefit. Oscar was disgusted with his step-daughter's choice in husband. He was even more disgusted by the fact that his grandson was not the "perfect" child he had anticipated. Oscar viewed the situation as a huge mess that reflected very poorly on him, and he was determined to make them all pay. Yes, Edith should have seen all of it coming, one way or another.

Edith was grateful for Giselle. Lord knew how Lawrence had found her, but evidently the woman had cleaned their house each week when they lived in Canada. Somehow he had convinced Oscar to bring her to the States and hire her as a full-time housekeeper. Why she had agreed, Edith wasn't sure, but she was now grateful. Giselle had stepped in where Xander's mother had failed. Giselle had held the household together as much as possible.

Edith liked her, which was saying a great deal. Although Edith had met many, many people on her travels, she liked few of them. Her expectations were high, and not many could meet them. That was fine with her. On the whole, she didn't like people very much anyway.

ॐ

Nicholas Black found it difficult to stay seated. He was cooped up in one of the police station's conference rooms trying to pay attention to the weekly briefing. His mind kept wandering, and he wanted nothing more than to stand up and start pacing.

At last the speaker stopped droning on and ended the meeting. Nick quickly stood. His partner beside him, Adam Johnson, stood as well. "All right there?" Johnson asked quietly.

Nick shot him a quizzical look.

"Never seen you fidget so much," Johnson said, knowing exactly what Nick was thinking.

Nick shook his head in reply. "Not now," he said. "I'll tell you later." He quickly walked out of the room and went straight to the front door of the station.

The rain had subsided to a heavy mist. He wasn't sure why, but Nick found it comforting. He shoved his hands in his pockets and made his way down the street.

He knew that he had no right to be thinking about her, but his mind was focused on Dulcie. Who had she been having coffee with? Was it a business meeting, or something more personal? Nick had only seen her companion's face for a few moments, but it was long enough to recognize that the man's interest was more than professional.

"Dammit," Nick muttered to himself. "Yeah, I really screwed things up. How am I going to fix this?" So far he had managed to turn his life around in terms of his career, but had accomplished little else. The rest seemed as though it was still a mess. True, he had extricated himself from a ridiculous marriage through an extremely prolonged divorce, but in the end it didn't seem like much of an accomplishment. At best, whenever he thought about it, and he tried very hard not to, it seemed like a trial. He had won; why then did he feel like he was the losing party?

Time. He had to keep reminding himself that time was the critical factor, and that he simply had to be patient. It was difficult for him. He desperately wanted to reestablish some sort of relationship with Dulcie. He deluded himself into believing that a simple friendship would suffice, but deep down he knew that it wouldn't. He was in love with her. There was nothing he could do about it. It gnawed at his heart.

He had no idea who the man was drinking coffee with Dulcie. It could easily have been a colleague. A simple work meeting. From the look on the man's face, however, Nick was inclined to believe otherwise. He knew that look. Unfortunately, he had not been able to see Dulcie's face, and she had rushed off so quickly that he had not been able to reposition himself so that he could observe her better. He snorted at the thought. He was thinking of the situation in terms of his police skills, using undercover observation on a stakeout. In reality, it could be considered borderline stalking.

He needed to refocus, to immerse himself in something that would take his mind off everything else.

Off her. He stopped and glanced behind him. Down the street, through the hazy mist, he saw the large bulk of his partner heading toward him. Nick waited for him to catch up. It was then that Nick remembered how Adam Johnson had problems of his own.

"How's the diet going?" Nick asked.

Johnson just glared at him.

"That good, eh?" Nick did sympathize. Plus, the look on Johnson's face was so pathetic, Nick abandoned all thoughts of poking fun at him. He wasn't in the mood, anyway. "Coffee?" It was nearby. Might as well get some.

"That's about all I consume these days anyway," Johnson said. "But one condition. I can't go in there." He nodded to the coffee shop down the street a few doors away from them. "You have to get it."

Nick's forehead wrinkled. "Mind if I ask why?"

Johnson sighed. "Think about it," he said, his feet firmly planted on the brick sidewalk. He wasn't going to budge one step closer.

Nick swiveled his head from Johnson back toward the plate-glass window of the coffee shop. Then it dawned on him. "Oh!" he said. This time he did laugh. "Too much temptation?"

"Yeah, you could say that," Johnson muttered.

Nick had remembered the array of pastries in the large display beneath the counter at this particular coffee shop. No amount of willpower would have kept his partner from caving to a sight like that. Nick even had trouble avoiding it, and pastries weren't his nemesis. "You wait here," he laughed. "I'll be right back."

Johnson nodded and muttered something as he attempted to become absorbed in the shop window beside him. It held various ladies' shoes and handbags. Definitely not enough of a distraction to keep his mind off the delectable treats down the street. His thoughts were detracted from food for a moment by some particularly odd and ugly shoes. Did women think they were attractive? He imagined someone wearing them, teetering along on the spindly high heels. He shook his head vigorously. Nope. Decidedly unattractive.

Nick came back as quickly as possible. They crossed the street and walked along in the direction of the ferry terminal. Nick knew that there would be few temptations of the culinary kind there. "So, have you dared get on the scale yet?" he asked.

Johnson shook his head as he swallowed. "Nope. I don't really want to until we're at the end. It's either going to be completely depressing or totally great. No sense in getting my hopes up. Or down, as the case may be."

Nick knew about getting his hopes up. He was silent for a few moments. "I talked with Dulcie's brother the other day," he said, changing the subject for his partner's sake.

Johnson knew exactly what Nick was really saying. He had watched the entire sequence of events between Dulcie and Nick unfold. He knew Nick was still interested. He also knew that, since Nick had not been completely straightforward with Dulcie about his own past, she now distrusted him. Johnson didn't think her attitude was completely without merit, but almost. Nick certainly had not intentionally misled her. He had simply been carried away by his feelings and probably should have kept them in check. Johnson couldn't blame him, though. The first time Adam Johnson had met his wife Maria, he thought his heart had stopped. He still felt that way, in spite of her current challenge. He would do anything for her, including spending a week at a weight-loss center and spa, although if he could avoid it he'd certainly try.

"Whadidya talk about?" Johnson asked.

"Not much. I just apologized. And I meant it."

"Think it worked?" Johnson said.

"Maybe. They're pretty close, as you know. He's protective of her. I can understand that. I just thought it was the right thing to do, talking to him."

Johnson nodded. "Never hurts to apologize, even if you don't need to." They had stopped walking and leaned against a railing, watching a big yellow and white ferry easily maneuver into its berth. Seagulls were circling it already, waiting to swoop in if departing passengers left any crumbs. "Did you apologize to her?" he asked.

Nick wrapped his hands around the still-warm paper cup. "I think so. I'm pretty sure I did. But I can't remember exactly when or what I said. It's all been a blur, especially with the last case." A few months earlier, a case involving an artist from the museum had thrown Dulcie and Nick together too quickly after she had learned about his messy divorce. They had worked together to solve the case, and he thought he had rebuilt some trust in the process, but since then he had heard nothing from her.

Johnson grimaced. "Sounds like you better be totally sure. 'Cause if you aren't, she sure as heck isn't, either."

"Good point," Nick replied. It was a good point, especially in light of what he had seen earlier through the window of the coffee shop, not to mention the potential competition that he might be facing in general.

"Don't wait around," Johnson said, turning his back to the ferry and leaning his large bulk against the railing.

"Yeah, you're right. I need to take the bull by the horns, don't I."

"Yep," Johnson said. "That and one other thing." He looked sideways at his partner.

"What's that?" Nick asked unhappily.

Johnson shoved himself away from the railing and began walking in the direction of the police station. "Don't get fat!" he called over his shoulder.

Nick had to grin. He needed that.

The knock on her door startled Edith. She had been deeply consumed in thought and didn't even know how long she had been standing there, staring out the window. "Yes?" she answered abruptly.

Giselle opened the door and poked her head in. "Call for you," she said quietly as she covered half of the phone with her hand. "Would you like to take it, or shall I tell them that you're busy?"

Edith shook her head. "Not busy. I'll take it," she barked, holding out her hand. Then she realized that the painting was easily seen behind her. Something told her that she should keep it to herself for the moment. She quickly walked toward Giselle and took the phone. Edith took another step toward Giselle who rapidly backed through the door, closing it behind her.

"Yes!" Edith announced. It was never a greeting, more of a declaration for the caller to get to the point.

"Mrs. Bernstein, this is Dulcie Chambers. I was wondering if I could arrange a time to come over with Dr. Raymond Armand and observe Xander while he works?"

"Why?" Edith demanded.

Dulcie had anticipated the question, although she was still surprised by Edith's tone. "As you so kindly agreed to let the museum film Xander," she began, "I want to make the best use of that time as possible. If I can observe him with the psychologist for a bit first, we can take up as little of his time as possible when the cameras are on him."

"You mean you'll be able to do it more cheaply," Edith countered.

Dulcie nearly laughed. Edith was blunt, but correct. "You're absolutely right. But it will take less of Xander's time as well, and be less of an intrusion overall."

"Fine. Come over tomorrow. He's usually in full swing in his studio by ten o'clock. You can have two hours with him, if it doesn't seem to affect him at all. If it does, you will leave."

"Yes, I understand," Dulcie said.

"I hope you're not expecting lunch," Edith replied.

This time Dulcie did laugh, but caught herself. "Not at all, Mrs. Bernstein. We'll try to be as inconspicuous as possible. Thank you so much for your time."

"Yes. I'll see you tomorrow, promptly at ten."

"Of course!" Dulcie managed to squeeze in before Edith's phone cut her off.

CHAPTER FIVE

"He has a truly single-minded focus," Raymond murmured to Dulcie. They had been sitting in a large window seat behind Xander as he worked. Raymond had been providing a running commentary as various thoughts about Xander occurred to him.

Dulcie had her laptop out and was taking notes. She was trying very hard not to respond to Raymond other than an occasional nod of acknowledgement. She felt it was rude to be talking about Xander right in front of him. Or actually, in this case, behind him.

Raymond sensed her uneasiness. "He can hear us, certainly, but does not process what we're saying. Imagine if you were sitting in a café and a couple seated behind you were speaking Italian. You wouldn't know if they were talking about you." He gave a lighthearted chuckle.

"Actually, I speak Italian," Dulcie replied flatly. It wasn't a lie. She wasn't fluent, but she certainly could carry on a general conversation. Just as it had before, his attitude was beginning to grate on her nerves. Besides, how did he really know whether or not Xander could understand them?

They both looked up as they heard bustling at the doorway. Giselle nudged the door open with her knee and came in with a tray loaded down with teacups and pastries. Dulcie looked at her gratefully. She couldn't know what a welcome interruption she was.

"Xander usually has tea now, and I thought you might like some as well," she smiled at Dulcie. She was careful not to make eye contact with Dr. Armand.

Xander put down his brush, walked to the tray, ate an entire scone, then poured a cup of tea. He took it back to his easel and stood, staring at the painting while he drank down the whole cup. Then he put it on the table beside him and began to work again.

Dulcie watched with interest. He had not requested assistance from Giselle in any way. She had not offered to help him, either. She simply stood back while he took what he needed. Yet, his actions did not seem impolite. Perhaps it was Giselle's complacent reaction, but Xander seemed to almost acknowledge her.

His manners were interesting, if they could be called manners. He was quite neat. He ate the scone without leaving a dusting of crumbs in front of him, something that Dulcie had difficulty doing at times. He drank the tea carefully, almost gently. Dulcie looked closely at him. His hair was brushed and looked clean. His clothes were obviously fresh and had little, if any, paint on them. Dulcie wondered how he had learned to be so careful. Was his father the same way?

She had the sudden urge to meet his father. Dulcie shook her head slightly at the thought, and realized that she was most likely thinking far too hard about this project. "No," she thought. "Focus on Xander, get the film crew in here, do the mini-documentary, and move on!" Yet her mind couldn't help but wander. How long was his father in prison? When would he be eligible for parole? Was Xander ever able to visit him? Did Xander miss him?

Dulcie's thoughts were interrupted by the clatter of a spoon hitting the floor. She looked over at Giselle. Raymond was helping himself to the tea tray, his back to Dulcie. Giselle quickly knelt to pick up the spoon and as she did, a look of anger briefly flitted across her face. She hissed something at Raymond who simply chuckled and turned away.

"*What was that?*" thought Dulcie. She realized that they must have known each other when Raymond had worked with Xander previously. Did they not get along? Perhaps he had done something to upset Giselle, or even Xander? Clearly Giselle was not enamored with Raymond. His affectedly charming demeanor was decidedly not working. It did not seem to bother him in the slightest, however.

As he turned around to rejoin Dulcie she felt a sudden chill fall across the room, as though a cloud of uneasiness had descended upon them all. Dulcie looked over at Xander. He had stopped painting. He walked toward the window and looked out. The day was bright and sunny, but a strong wind howled off the ocean. Dulcie had never liked windy days. They always made her feel angry.

Since Xander was not working she decided to take a break herself and get some tea. She closed her laptop and carefully put it back in her briefcase just as Raymond had reached his seat. He sat as she stood. It seemed slightly awkward. She smiled to cover her thoughts, knowing full well that he could see through them.

Giselle had joined Xander at the window. They were both silent. She looked at him and brought her hand to her mouth, as though drinking. He remained still, not acknowledging her. Then, still looking out the window, he slowly raised his own hand to his mouth as she had just done. Giselle's eyes widened. She went back to the tea tray and refilled his cup, leaving it on the table beside his painting. Several moments later, Xander went back to his easel, drank down all of the tea, then picked up his paintbrush.

As Giselle collected his cup, she made a quick motion to Dulcie with her head. Dulcie understood. She followed Giselle across the room. Giselle busied herself clattering cups and spoons, so that no one could hear. She leaned over to Dulcie and whispered, "He has not communicated back to me like that since his father was sent away!"

Dulcie suddenly remembered that Xander had communicated with her, or she believed that he had. The first time that she had seen him work, when she had asked him for the painting, he had held his hand open, with palm up. She took it as a gesture of giving. "Giselle, has he ever done this," she made the gesture, "with you before?"

Giselle looked surprised. "Yes, but again, not for quite some time. How could you know that?"

Raymond now joined them. "Am I correct in noticing that our friend has begun communicating again?"

"Yes, we think so," said Dulcie.

Raymond looked over at Xander. "That is very good. It's an excellent sign that the healing process is underway with him. He's able to reach out to others again, or at the very least, respond to them. It is his own way of reaching out, I suppose."

"Does he ever respond to people that he doesn't know?" asked Dulcie.

"Not that I have ever seen," said Giselle.

"Of course he can," Raymond began, but was interrupted by Giselle.

"*Non!* That ees *not* what she asked!" the housekeeper snapped, her French Canadian accent deepening.

Dulcie looked back and forth between the two. How well did they know each other? She knew that Raymond had certainly been in the house when he had worked with Xander. Did he simply get on Giselle's nerves, or was there something else?

Giselle turned to Dulcie, "You must excuse me. I have been with the boy since he was a baby. I have become protective of him, perhaps overly so."

Raymond chuckled behind her but said nothing. Dulcie saw Giselle's back stiffen but she remained silent as well.

Dulcie cleared her throat. "Well then, I suppose we have seen enough for today. We should probably give Xander some space and let him continue his work in peace."

"Yes, and I must get back to my office for an appointment," Raymond interjected.

Good, Dulcie thought. She wanted to speak to Giselle alone. She hung back as Raymond left, letting Giselle shut the door behind him, perhaps more firmly than necessary. Dulcie took her time with her coat, waiting to hear Raymond's car door shut, then she turned to Giselle. "May I be blunt?" she asked.

Relief seemed to wash over Giselle. "Yes, perhaps that is best at this point!"

"How well does he really know Xander?" Dulcie jerked her head toward the now closed door. "How much time did he spend in the house?"

Giselle paused, not sure how much to reveal. The correct answer was that Raymond had spent a great deal of time in the house, but only half of that time was with Xander. She decided that the correct answer was not necessary, however. Not now, at any rate. "Our Dr. Armand is a man *très intéressant*," Giselle replied, dodging Dulcie's latter question. "As I'm sure you have noticed. I believe that he does understand Xander, but as a… what is the word… specimen?"

"Do you mean, an example of someone with his condition, rather than an individual?" Dulcie asked.

"Yes, yes! That is exactly what I mean. *Dr. Armand*," she stressed his title as though there were some mistruth to it, "Sees only how he may gain from a situation. In Xander's case, he wanted to study him and write scientific papers to publish. He told me once that it would benefit his career."

Well that explains a lot! Dulcie thought. To Raymond, Xander was simply a case study. Yet, wouldn't that be true with nearly anyone brought in to evaluate the boy? She decided to change the subject. "Could I see the rest of the house, Giselle? I need to bring a film crew in here, and I want them to interrupt your lives as little as possible."

Giselle nodded with understanding. "Yes, of course. Follow me," she said as she quickly led the way down the hall. "You have been in the living room, I believe." She gestured as they walked by a doorway. Dulcie had, the day of her brief meeting and cup of tea with Edith Bernstein. "We have a powder room here," she waved at a small space under the large staircase, "Then the kitchen back here," She stepped into a gleaming, white room.

Dulcie blinked. The walls were the color of cream, as was the stove and massive porcelain sink. The marble countertops were streaked with veins of gray, the only contrast in the bright room. Yet it did not come across as sterile or stark. *Soft*, was the word that leapt into Dulcie's mind. It reminded her of a Michelangelo sculpture, the way he was able to make a massive, hard block of stone look as though it was warm and supple.

Giselle was still speaking. "Do you know if your *cinema* people will require meals?" she asked, concluding a sentence that Dulcie had not heard.

"Oh! That's a very good question. I have no idea, but I will find out. I'll give you a complete schedule of what to expect. I'm truly hoping that we intrude on your lives as little as possible." Dulcie said with sincerity.

The two continued up the stairs. They passed a door that stood ajar. Giselle paused. "You may as well look in there," she said, slowly pushing open the door. She stopped in the doorway and turned to face Dulcie. "It is where the old man died. Or rather, where he was pushed from the window. I suppose he would have actually expired on the ground below." She grimaced.

Dulcie looked beyond her and into the room. Heavy curtains framed large, multi-paned French windows. Unlike Xander's studio, these did not have a window seat beneath them. They reached nearly to the floor. A heavy oak desk stood in the middle of the room, close to the windows.

Dulcie was silent for a moment as she looked around the room. It appeared to be unused and had a depressingly overbearing feeling about it. Without warning, Dulcie shivered.

"Yes, it makes me do that too," Giselle said quietly.

Before she could stop herself, Dulcie blurted out, "Giselle, what happened? I know that you weren't here, but what do you think really happened?"

The other woman shook her head. "I wish I knew," she said without looking at Dulcie. "But I do know one thing. He was an evil man," she said.

Dulcie's eyes widened.

"Yes," Giselle continued. "He delighted in tormenting others. He would play games to make everyone feel uncomfortable. He could find your weakness, and before you knew what was happening, he would slide his words into that part of your mind like a knife through the heart. No one was safe, not even his own daughter. That is why she drank so much, I believe. The only person that he could not hurt was Xander, because no one can know what is in his mind. I think that is the single thing that tormented Oscar Bernstein, the fact that there was one person he could not control."

"Why did everyone stay?" asked Dulcie. "Wouldn't they have been better off not living in such a situation?"

Giselle sighed. "Certainly they would have been, but they stayed for many reasons. Xander was not always as self-reliant as he is now. Imagine him as a young boy, unable to communicate, not knowing how to dress or bathe or even eat properly. He required a great deal of professional therapy and care, all of which costs money. The only person with enough money to provide everything was the old man. And he paid all of the bills, with only the one condition: they all must live in this house."

"I think I can guess the rest," Dulcie replied. "They had no idea what they were getting themselves into, and Oscar Bernstein's interference was a slow, insidious process."

Giselle frowned as she replied, "Very slow and very insidious. It is the best way to describe it."

Dulcie wondered how Giselle had retained her own sanity throughout the process.

"I can see your thoughts," Giselle spoke quietly.

Dulcie opened her mouth to speak, then closed it quickly.

Giselle continued, "You are thinking, *how could Giselle escape the torment when the others could not?* The answer is quite simple. First, as a servant, I can remain invisible. Second, also as a servant, I learn everyone's secrets. Everyone has them. Secrets. Most are of no consequence." She waved her hand in the air as if to discount them en masse. "But some, some are quite important. Oscar Bernstein had one of those, and I knew what it was. Perhaps it was less of a secret than a weakness, but he did not want anyone to know, nonetheless."

"What was it?" Dulcie asked, knowing that she should really not be so curious.

Giselle laughed. "I will tell you. It does not matter now. The old man was, as you can imagine, quite vain. He was the, I do not know it in your language, *narcissique?*"

"Narcissist, in English" Dulcie replied. "But that would have been fairly obvious I should think," she said quizzically.

"*Certainement*, but it leads to his secret. You see, he was very ashamed and I believe even disgusted by Xander. Monsieur Bernstein could not accept that he had such a grandson. It was the other reason that he kept them all in this house. The fewer who knew about his *disgrace*, the better. I saw him look at Xander many times with eyes of loathing."

Dulcie could only imagine how dysfunctional the entire family must have been. She was glad that Xander was unable to recognize his grandfather's feelings. Yet, was that true? Was he unaware, or did he simply show no emotion?

Their conversation was interrupted by the domineering presence of Edith Bernstein entering the room.

"Good, you haven't left yet. Come with me," she commanded looking at Dulcie. Giselle was clearly ignored in the statement. The housekeeper turned away, giving Dulcie a bemused smile as she left.

"Of course, Mrs. Bernstein. Is there something you wanted me to see?"

"Obviously," barked the older woman.

They continued farther down the corridor, away from the stairs. As they passed by Xander's studio, Dulcie saw him painting again.

Edith led Dulcie into her bedroom and quietly shut the door. "Earlier I was cleaning up some things of Xander's. He has all of those paintings just standing there in the studio, and I decided they needed organizing. While I was moving them, I found this," she pointed to the painting that she had found earlier, now propped up on the chair in the window. "Have a look and tell me what you see."

Dulcie stepped forward. She looked intently. Two men appeared to have been talking. One was leaving the room, looking distraught. The other was laughing meanly, or perhaps sneering? Or both? She glanced at Edith Bernstein. "Who are these men?" she asked.

"Oscar, and his son Lawrence," the woman replied curtly. "Look closer. Anything else you see? Is there anyone else?"

Dulcie peered again at the painting. "No one I can see, but there is a shadow, over here," she pointed.

"Good, good," Edith nodded, muttering quietly.

"But I don't think I understand why you would show me…" she was cut off by the other woman.

"Those were the clothes Oscar was wearing the night he was killed. That's the window he fell through," she pointed to the canvas directly behind him. "It appears to be about the time of day that he was killed, at dusk," Edith barked.

The significance began to dawn on Dulcie. "Xander made this painting," she said. It was a statement, not a question.

"Of course," Edith responded.

"And he only paints what he sees," Dulcie continued.

"Now you're getting it," the older woman said.

"So, there must have been another person in the study with Oscar Bernstein. Another person in the house."

"Exactly," Edith acknowledged. "It wouldn't have been Giselle. She never went in Oscar's study, unless he wasn't even in the house. She hates the room. Supposedly, Lawrence was the only other person in the house. This seems to show otherwise." She boomed.

"Yes, it does," Dulcie said. "But Mrs. Bernstein, I don't understand why you're showing this to me, specifically."

Edith walked across the room. She shot back over her shoulder, "I took the painting from Xander's study earlier. He was there. He knows I have it. I left this room for a little while. When I came back, this was sitting on the floor propped up against the chair. I think he's trying to tell us something." Edith picked up another canvas and turned it around to face Dulcie.

She was now staring at a portrait of herself.

CHAPTER SIX

Dulcie paced up and down the length of her office at the Maine Museum of Art. She knew what she had to do. She had to call Nick. She had to tell him about the painting. It could change everything about Lawrence Bellamy's conviction. Her history with Nick, however, was a consternation. He hadn't exactly lied to her, but he hadn't told the truth, either. She wanted to distance herself from him until she could sort out her own feelings. Fate, however, seemed to have other plans in mind.

She turned and, with head down, quickly strode back across the room. She nearly ran straight into the bottle-cap Statue of Liberty. "Dammit!" she swore under her breath, sidestepping at the last second.

Without giving herself another moment to change her mind, she picked up her phone, located Nick's number, and pressed the call button.

It rang several times. She was about to hang up without leaving a message when he answered.

"Dulcie?"

She was silent, not sure what to say.

"Is that you?" she heard him say. "Dulcie, are you okay?"

She inhaled slowly. "Yes, it's me, Nick. Yes, I'm fine. I just wanted to talk to you about something that's, well, odd." She stopped abruptly.

Nick was instantly concerned. "Dulcie, are you in any trouble?"

Now she laughed. She was being entirely too serious, and nervous, about talking with him. After all she was, in her professional capacity, simply conveying some important information to him, a police detective in his professional capacity. No need for silly feelings, really, she told herself. Without realizing it she stood up straight.

"No, Nick, I'm not in any kind of trouble. I just wanted to talk with you about something odd that I think the Police should know of."

Now Nick was silent. She hadn't called him for any personal reasons. It was strictly business. What else could he expect? "Sure, Dulcie. Go ahead."

"I can't explain it very well over the phone. It's something that you have to see. Could you and Adam come by my office sometime today when it's convenient?"

You and Adam. He knew what that meant. She didn't want to see him alone. She wanted Nick's partner, Adam Johnson, there also.

"We can be there this afternoon. Does two o'clock work for you?" Nick asked.

"That's perfect. I'll see you then," she said and quickly ended the call. She sank into her chair. *Whew - that was done.*

Rachel poked her head around the door. "Fresh pot of coffee! Want some?"

"Seriously, you'll get me coffee?" Dulcie exclaimed.

Rachel giggled. "Well, it's not on the job description, but you look like you need it. Hang on." She was back in two minutes with a steaming mug. As she handed it to Dulcie she saw the new painting by Xander Bellamy with Oscar Bernstein and his son. She cocked her head sideways, looking at it. "That's the same guy who did that one," she pointed at the portrait of Dulcie. "Isn't it?"

"Good eye!" Dulcie praised. "I'm training you well!"

Rachel now rolled her eyes.

"Tell me what you see," Dulcie added.

Rachel gazed very intently at the painting. Dulcie had been serious in giving her the compliment. Her assistant had a very good eye for detail. Dulcie waited, patiently silent.

At last Rachel stepped back. "He," she pointed at Oscar Bernstein, "... is a total ass. And he," she pointed at Lawrence Bellamy, "... is really annoyed. No wait, that's not the right word. Dismayed? Yes, that's closer. He looks like his whole world is caving in on him." Rachel looked back at Dulcie. "Who are they?" she asked.

Dulcie was processing Rachel's assessment. It summed everything up quite neatly. After a moment she said, "The 'total ass' is Oscar Bernstein, and the dismayed one is his son-in-law, Lawrence Bellamy."

"The guy who pushed Xander's grandfather out the window?" Rachel squeaked in surprise.

"Yes. Strange, isn't it?" observed Dulcie.

"Yeah, I'll say!" Rachel exclaimed. Something about the painting was oddly frightening although she could not decide what it was.

"I have a meeting at two, with detectives from the police. They want to have a look at this," Dulcie said. She tried to be as casual as possible.

Rachel turned to her. "With that dishy detective? Nicholas Black? He's got the hots for you!" she declared.

"That's enough," Dulcie huffed. "Yes, if you must know, it's with him *and* his partner, Adam Johnson, and it's strictly business. So don't go getting any ideas or spreading any gossip," she concluded.

Rachel said nothing but left the room whistling softly, taunting her boss.

"I could fire you, you know!" Dulcie called after her.

"But you won't!" Rachel jested quietly in a song-song voice from outside the door.

Dulcie grinned.

At two o'clock Dulcie heard a soft tapping at her office door. She quickly slipped on the black pumps that she had kicked off under her desk. Her heels clicked across the floor as she crossed the room, pulling open the door.

"Thanks for coming," she said to both Nicholas Black and Adam Johnson as a general greeting. She wanted to address them as a group. She had vowed not to engage in an individual conversation with Nick.

She had no reason to avoid him, really. He hadn't actually done anything wrong. True, her pride had been bruised, but looking back, he had simply been kind toward her, only bordering on affectionate. She was sure he had not intentionally 'led her on' as the phrase went, yet he had not been straightforward as to his own status and availability. He had been married. Technically, he had been separated and going through an overly prolonged divorce, but none of this information had been provided. As a result, she had begun to develop feelings for him, only to have them snuffed out by an embarrassing encounter with his soon-to-be-ex-wife. Dulcie still felt like a complete idiot every time she thought about it.

She refocused on the two men standing in the doorway and stepped aside, motioning for them to come in.

"So this has to do with that Bernstein case?" Johnson asked. Dulcie was glad he had spoken first and not Nick.

"Yes," she said, looking directly at Johnson. "I realize the case is closed, that Lawrence Bellamy confessed, but I've had reason to talk with the family.

I've even been to the house a couple of times. It's just that everything seems odd."

Nick and his partner exchanged glances. They had used the exact same word on the way over when talking about the case.

Dulcie continued. "I've been putting together a new exhibit, and wanted to feature some of Xander Bellamy's work. I'm sure you know about his talents. He's an autistic savant with an eidetic memory."

Johnson's brow wrinkled. "Do you mean a photographic memory?"

"Basically yes, although no one has yet proven that the concept of a photographic memory truly exists. An eidetic memory is the ability to recall what has been seen, or in some cases heard, with extreme precision for a time afterward. A small percentage of very young children, five years old or less, have it but it seems to fade when language skills develop. In Xander's case, he may have maintained the ability since he has no language skills."

"Interesting…" murmured Nick.

"Here's a painting that Xander did of me after he had seen me for only a few minutes," she walked over to the portrait of herself. "I was standing behind him when he actually painted it, so he was not looking at me at all while he painted." The two men followed her and stared at the canvas.

"It's so detailed, and looks exactly like you," Nick remarked.

"Wow," Johnson simply stated.

"The point is, Xander takes in an image, a scene, a person, then paints exactly what he has seen. Rather quickly, too." Dulcie reached for the other painting and turned it around. She had deliberately placed it against the wall so that the men couldn't see it when they first came in. "Edith Bernstein, Oscar Bernstein's sister, gave this to me, knowing that I would show it to you. Tell me what you see."

The two men leaned forward and bumped each other on the shoulders. Johnson grunted and stepped back slightly. He fished for his glasses in his shirt pocket and put them on. "Looks like an old man with a maniacal laugh, and a pretty upset guy walking away from him."

Nick was silent.

Johnson straightened and turned back to Dulcie. "I'm assuming the older one is Oscar Bernstein and the younger is Lawrence Bellamy?"

"Yes," Dulcie replied. "How did you know?"

"Well, otherwise you wouldn't be showing it to us," he said with a smirk. "But seriously, what's the story?"

Nick, still silent, stood up as well and faced Dulcie.

"Here's what happened. I'm planning to video Xander as he works as kind of a mini-documentary for the upcoming exhibit. I was at the house this morning to observe him and to just get an idea of how things are situated so that I can cause the least amount of intrusion. While the housekeeper was showing me around, Edith Bernstein caught up with us and asked me to look at this painting. She said that it shows both Oscar and Lawrence Bellamy in the same clothes that they wore the night Oscar was killed, and judging form the light outside the window, it shows them right around the same time that he was killed, just before sunset."

"So Xander saw them right before it happened?" Johnson asked. "That doesn't really tell us anything, does it? Why would Edith give it to you?"

Dulcie was thoughtful. "For two reasons. First of all, the painting shows something interesting. A shadow of someone else in the room. It's right here," she pointed. "Secondly, she had found this painting in Xander's studio. He has stacks of his discarded works in there. He was in the studio when she found it and must have been aware that she brought it back to her room. Later, Edith found another painting of me, one that Xander had done previously, also in her room next to this one. She believes that Xander was trying to convey that she should show the painting to me."

"Seems odd," said Johnson taking off his glasses.

Nick finally spoke. "I looked over the Bernstein file before we came over. There were four people at home when Oscar was killed: Oscar himself, his son-in-law Lawrence, the housekeeper, and Xander. Evidence pointed to Xander at first, but then Lawrence stepped forward and confessed. He said that the housekeeper had taken Xander for a walk. When they were gone, the two men had argued, and in anger, Lawrence shoved him out the window." Nick glanced back at the painting. "I don't mean to sound disrespectful, but I don't see that this disproves any of that."

Dulcie shook her head. "It doesn't really. But it does seem strange. Who is the other person in the room? I doubt it would have been Giselle. She's the housekeeper," Dulcie added. Both men nodded. "The whole thing struck Edith Bernstein as strange, too. Plus, why would Xander want me to see it?"

"You don't think this kid was just using artistic license? I mean, maybe he walked by the room and saw some of this, but just put the rest in?" Johnson asked.

"No. That's not how his mind works. He only paints what he sees. He doesn't create a scene, he captures an image. No, someone else was definitely there."

Nick felt an odd, prickly sensation creeping up his neck. He reached back and rubbed beneath his collar. Dulcie was right. Something seemed very strange about the whole scenario. He pulled out his cell phone. "Mind if I take a picture of this for reference?" he asked.

"Be my guest," said Dulcie as she moved out of the way. Nick took several photos with his phone.

Johnson cleared his throat. "Guess I'll have a look at that file too. Nick, you sure no one else was around when it happened?"

"Yeah, that's what it said," Nick replied, refocusing on a close-up of Oscar Bernstein.

"We can't exactly go around asking questions. Case is closed, so no one would go for that." Johnson was thinking out loud.

"You couldn't, but I could," said Dulcie. Both men wheeled around and stared at her.

"Look, Dulcie," Nick started, "I know you've helped with other investigations, but it might not be a good idea…"

Now Dulcie was annoyed. She had not only 'helped' with other investigations, she had actually been instrumental in solving them. She knew that it was probably some sort of misplaced male protective instinct that made Nick hesitate, but she wasn't about to allow him to tell her what she could or couldn't say to these people. "Fine," she lied.

Johnson chuckled. "Now see what you've done," he said in a stage-whisper to Nick. "No tellin' what she'll do now, but she sure as heck isn't gonna let this drop!" He continued at normal volume, "Think about it, though. She is in the best position to get a little more information. Plus, if nothing is conclusive, we can just let the whole thing go."

Nick sighed. He knew that Johnson was right. "Okay, Dulcie. You win. But let us," he nodded at his partner, "talk about this first and figure out exactly what we need to know. I'll be in touch. *Please* don't try to find out anything on your own in the meantime?"

Dulcie smiled sweetly. "Of course not, sir!"

Nick groaned inwardly.

Detective Nicholas Black and his partner walked back down the street toward the police station. Nick zipped his leather jacket higher on his chest. Fall had definitely begun to chill the air. "So what do you make of that?" he said to Johnson without looking at him.

"I think you better start making some moves, or she won't know you're still interested."

Nick sighed. "I mean…"

Johnson grinned. "Yeah, I know what you mean."

They were approaching their unofficial second office, the coffee shop Roasters. "Wanna get a coffee?" Nick asked.

Johnson stopped dead in his tracks. "I can't go in there," he stammered.

Nick suddenly remembered Johnson's bet with his wife. "Oh, I forgot! Sorry. Want me to grab us a couple of coffees? I'll just bring them back out."

"That'd be great. Thanks."

"Should I ask how the diet is going?" Nick said as they approached the front steps of Roasters.

"No," Johnson said flatly.

Nick left it at that.

When he came back out, Johnson was coming back down the street in the same direction that they had just walked. Nick chuckled softly. "Getting the extra steps in?" he asked, handing Johnson a large, very warm cup.

"Might as well," his partner said, shrugging his shoulders.

They crossed the street and headed for the ferry terminal. Outdoors, but covered from the weather, it was a good place to sit and think. They found an empty bench and sipped their coffee in silence.

A loud blast from a departing boat interrupted Nick's thoughts. He looked over at it, watching the seagulls swooping dangerously close, but never actually hitting anything. He'd always marveled at how birds could do that. His mind drifted back to the Bernstein case. It was the same thing. All of the suspects had been flitting around, near the crime but not close enough to pin any of them down. It had all seemed so strange to him.

"We're gonna have to get at the files again and go through everything," Johnson said. Nick nodded in response. "Chief won't be happy," Johnson added.

"You've got that right. He likes a tidy finish so he can move on. We'll have to just keep it as quiet as possible," Nick replied.

Johnson finished his coffee with one large swig, then tossed the cup into the trash can about ten feet away. It bounced off the rim, but went in. He gestured two fingers, points for the basket. Johnson was a kid at heart. One corner of Nick's mouth tugged up in a half-smile, but it was his only acknowledgement.

"What's your gut?" Johnson asked.

"Good question. My gut says that Lawrence Bellamy didn't do it. We both agree on that. But your real question is, who do I think did? Damned if I don't have a good answer to that. That painting is interesting. The kid isn't stupid, he just thinks differently. What I don't know is, is he really trying to tell us something with that image, or is it just something random he did showing the night that his grandfather just happened to be killed?"

"My gut says it isn't random. He did it for a reason. He also got it to Dulcie for a reason. We just don't know what that reason is."

"That's what we need to figure out," Nick said. The last inch of his coffee was cold. He stood up and dropped the cup in the trash. "All right, let's get back and start digging."

Johnson grunted in agreement.

❧

Dr. Raymond Armand sprinkled a small quantity of aftershave on his hands, rubbed them together, then slapped them on his cheeks. He was meeting Dulcie for dinner and decided to be ready for anything. He had called her earlier in the day, telling her that he had been so busy with appointments that the only time he had available to talk about the project would be over dinner. Of course, there had been no appointments at all during the day. He simply intended to mix business with pleasure.

His file on Xander Bellamy was sitting on the desk. Dr. Armand had just read through the contents again. As far as he was concerned, it seemed pretty standard, if an autistic savant could be considered standard. Xander had been diagnosed at an early age. Thanks to his grandfather's money, he had received a great deal of therapy. Raymond knew that the earlier therapy happened, the better, and that had certainly been true in Xander's case. He'd learned enough life skills, such as feeding himself properly, hygiene, dressing, etc., to function well. Raymond thought about his plan to make a case study of Xander, publishing the results in one of the Boston medical journals for psychology. The grandfather had interfered. When Oscar Bernstein learned of Raymond's plans, he was immediately dismissed. To Oscar, his grandson was nothing more than a disgrace. Oscar had only paid for the therapy in an attempt to make him "normal" and less of what he considered to be an embarrassment. It hadn't worked to his satisfaction. He wanted as few people to know about Xander as possible.

Raymond had been livid. Publishing his own case study would have been a big step in his career. His name would be linked to Xander's. It could have led to more studies of Xander and others like him, followed by more publications. He had imagined giving lectures to his so called 'esteemed colleagues,' the very same people who had snubbed him so recently before. Oscar Bernstein had certainly thrown a wrench into Raymond's career.

He glanced at the file again, debating whether he should bring it with him. It probably wasn't a bad idea. At the very least, it would make a convincing prop, showing that he was there for business. And if something else just happened to develop, well, that was certainly acceptable. He had every intention of ensuring that something else did indeed develop. Dulcie was well connected. She would be very useful. The fact that she was quite easy on the eyes was a serious bonus.

He shoved the file into his buttery leather briefcase, checked to make sure he had a pair of reading glasses in with it as well, then left the office. They were meeting at a trendy new restaurant, the Seaglass Bistro. He arrived early and secured a table at the edge of one of the large windows. He was careful not to place them too far back into a dark corner. That would be too obvious.

Dulcie arrived within ten minutes. Raymond immediately stood and, when she had attempted a standard handshake, took her hand gently in his, placing his other hand on top. He then slid her coat from her shoulders. She immediately felt uncomfortable.

Raymond handed the coat to a nearby waiter without even acknowledging him. The man looked momentarily bewildered, then put it on a hook on the wall within easy reach of them. He gave each of them menus and was about to relate the chef's specials when Raymond interrupted. "I believe the lady would like some refreshment. If I may be so bold," he hesitated, glancing at Dulcie. Inwardly, she was not amused, but simply gave him a slight smile and nodded. "A glass of prosecco for each of us, if you will. Your best, if you don't mind." He then turned his attention to Dulcie, obviously dismissing the waiter by ignoring him. "We'll see if this place is as good as it claims to be," he said, knowing that the waiter could easily hear him.

Dulcie was amazed that someone whose career was devoted to understanding the thoughts of others could be so oblivious to their feelings. She quickly realized, however, that he was not oblivious at all. He simply didn't care. She reached into her bag and took out a small notepad and pen. They were meeting for work, not to review the restaurant.

"I wonder if you've had any thoughts regarding the best way to approach telling Xander's story? We'll need to be as brief as possible," she added.

"We will, and we'll need to make sure that it's in terms that the lay-public can understand. I guess that means I'll simply have to dumb it down quite a bit," Raymond sniffed.

This is going to be the longest dinner I've ever had,' Dulcie thought. Aloud she said, "I thought we could begin by showing his subject, the camera moving around him or her, then pull back and show that person sitting behind Xander. The camera could then move to a close-up of the canvas as he works, gradually pulling back as you explain his condition. He works so quickly that I think we could give our audience the essence of what he does in about five minutes."

The waiter had just returned with the drinks. Raymond was examining his closely. He froze with it hovering in the air. "Five minutes? That's all? I don't see how one could explain the complexity of his condition in five minutes!" he gaped. "Especially to the general public who have no real understanding of how the mind works." He trailed off, refocusing on his prosecco. He took a sip and made a face. "Passable," he sneered.

Dulcie looked up at the waiter and gave him a bright smile. "I'm just going to order an appetizer; I really don't have time for an entire dinner. The crab cakes sound delicious."

"Very good. I'll put that right in. And for you sir?" the waiter asked, turning to Raymond.

He was caught off guard. "Weren't we having dinner?" he stammered.

"I'm so sorry, I didn't get a chance to mention it when I came in, but I have a conference call with a colleague in Los Angeles. It's at half-past three, Pacific Time, so I'll have to dash off in," she looked at her tiny gold watch, "less than an hour!" Her eyes widened in surprise. She hoped she had fooled him.

He cleared his throat. The waiter was still standing over them. Raymond did not want to look like a fool in front of him. "Certainly! My schedule has been simply packed as well," he recovered and glanced at the menu. "I'll have the calamari in puttanesca." He flipped the menu back toward the waiter.

Dulcie sipped her prosecco. "Is this the La Marca?" She asked the waiter.

He flashed a surprised smile. "Yes, it is. Do you like it?"

"Absolutely! The melon really comes through in this vintage. Thanks so much for choosing it for us." She wanted him to know that at least one person at the table had manners. Plus, Dulcie knew her wines. It was a hobby bordering on a passion. She usually kept quiet with her knowledge, not wanting to come across as arrogant, but in this case Dr. Raymond Armand needed to be taken down a notch. He fixed his gaze out the window, pretending to be distracted by the street traffic.

When the waiter left, Dulcie said nothing, allowing silence to descend upon them. After several increasingly awkward moments, Raymond said, "Yes, you were telling me about the video. Where do you see my role? What would you like me to do?" He had quickly decided to hand her the reigns entirely or he was in danger of losing the project.

She toyed with the pen on her notepad. "I had thought that if you narrate, essentially through a voice-over, that would give it the level of professionalism, from a psychological standpoint, that we need."

"I would be happy to," he said simply, inwardly relieved.

"I do have some questions about Xander. First of all, how do we know that he'll paint the subject that we put in front of him?"

Raymond looked truly thoughtful for the first time since Dulcie had joined him at the table. "We don't. What I mean to say is, we can't be sure that he will. He paints what he wants to paint."

"He seems to be communicating again. Is there a way to ask him to paint someone? Has anyone tried communicating that before?"

"I don't think so. Xander has been given free reign with his painting."

"That leads me to another question. How did he learn to paint?" Dulcie asked.

"From what I understand," Raymond answered, "it was part of his therapy when he was very young. They used tempera paints with him. His skills were astonishing, so he eventually advanced to the oil paints that he uses now."

'*Acrylics*,' thought Dulcie. '*Not oils*.' She decided not to correct him.

"I think what I'd like to have you describe is the workings of a typical person's brain in terms of what they see and how they recreate it on paper or canvas, then describe what you believe is happening in Xander's brain."

"Would I do this while he's working?" Raymond asked.

"Initially, yes," Dulcie said. "But mainly that's to get your impressions as he works. Then we'll work out a script and do the voice-over for the final video."

"You've done this before, I see," Raymond observed.

"A couple of times," she answered.

As their food arrived, Dulcie realized that when Raymond let his guard down and stopped acting the part of the 'brilliant scientist' he was actually quite interesting. They continued talking until Dulcie glanced at her watch and realized that she had to leave for her fictitious phone call. She quickly reached into her bag and took out her wallet.

"No, no!" Raymond waved her off. "This is on me!"

Dulcie had no intention of letting him pay. "Thank you, but I couldn't let you. It's work, after all. Here," she said, laying cash on the table, "We'll split it. But I don't have time to wait for the check. Do you mind handling it?"

"With pleasure."

Dulcie wondered how it could be a pleasure to sit and wait for the check, but didn't ask. Raymond stood and helped her with her coat. His hands lingered on her shoulders a bit too long. She stepped away quickly and stuck out her hand formally, then managed a firm, quick handshake with him. "Thank you. I think we have plenty to work with now. I'll be in touch."

As she closed the door behind her and stepped onto the sidewalk, Dulcie initially turned toward the street she lived on, then quickly remembered that she was supposed to be on the phone with her imaginary colleague back at the office. She switched course, grateful that she was not walking in front of the window where Raymond still sat, although she was sure, somehow, that he was watching her.

She was regretting bringing him in to the whole project. Surely she could have found someone else. Yet he did have a history with Xander, so he would be able to give the needed insights in the least amount of time possible. She knew the phrase *time is money* all too well. The budget for the entire exhibit seemed to be sifting through her fingers. She couldn't afford to pay Dr. Raymond Armand for any longer than was absolutely necessary.

When she was well away from the restaurant, Dulcie turned down a side street and pulled out her cell phone. She pushed the number for her favorite Chinese restaurant and ordered a large chicken fried rice with two egg rolls. Then she pocketed the phone and continued on her way. '*Good!*' she thought. '*Now I can look forward to dinner!*'

CHAPTER SEVEN

Rain swept in from the ocean in sheets the following morning. Giselle watched it hammer at the window as she drank her coffee. It was the cold, thick, dark rain that she liked. To her, it felt as though it formed protective walls around everything. Did she still need the walls? She had put up so many in her life. Some were for her alone, but most were for others. Especially Xander.

From the moment she had first seen him, she knew he was special. He had not yet been diagnosed, but she knew. Her bond with him was instantaneous and permanent. She loved him as she would have her own child.

Her own child. It would never be. She had been told long ago that she was barren. The doctor had given her all of the medical jargon to explain her condition, but it didn't matter. The outcome was the same whether or not she understood why.

She was not a woman who yearned for a baby anyway. Babies grow up. They become children, then teenagers, then adults. They develop their own personalities. Simply because you are related doesn't mean that they will be nice. It doesn't mean they will like you, or even respect you.

What she did yearn for, and what she received from Xander, was a purpose for living. He needed her. She needed him, too. He gave her a reason to get up each morning.

She looked around the kitchen, soft and dark on the rainy morning. She should turn the lights on. Someone else would be coming down soon.

Giselle remembered the times when *he* came down. The old man. He stamped down the stairs and typically snarled something at her. She had learned to ignore it. When he wasn't snarling he was leering. She had also learned to stay out of arms reach. To be grabbed or, even worse, cornered by Oscar Bernstein was somewhere between unpleasant and horrifying.

Yet that wasn't why she had hated him. She hated him because of his disgust for Xander, his only grandchild. The only reason Xander was under this roof was to keep him from being seen by the rest of the world. The only reason that Oscar Bernstein had paid huge sums of money for therapy was to *'make that ridiculous fool of a child stop being an idiot'* as Oscar would say over and over, even with Xander in front of him. Xander never reacted, but Giselle knew that, at some level, he understood. He must have. Giselle's hatred had burned for many years. She was glad it was over. She was glad he was dead.

A soft footstep pulled her away from her thoughts. Xander had padded into the kitchen in his slippers. He stopped in the middle of the room and stared out the window. Giselle waited. Sometimes he sat at the table. When he did that, she knew it was scrambled eggs. Sometimes he walked to the counter. On those days it was just toast. Yet today he did neither. He simply looked out the window at the rain. He stood, motionless, for a very long time. Then he turned and left.

Giselle was a bit surprised. Perhaps he wasn't hungry? She would bring him up something in a little while. Now she heard a sturdy clomping on the stairs. Edith. Giselle did not dislike Edith. Although they were immensely different, they had a shared motivation. Both would not allow any harm to come to Xander.

Edith stepped into the kitchen and immediately flicked on the light. "Sitting in the dark? That won't do. Encourages brooding!" She marched over to the coffee pot, poured out a cup and drank half of it down. She refilled the cup and went to the table where Giselle sat.

Scraping out a chair and hefting herself into it, she plunked down the cup. "How's the boy today?" she asked. "Saw him on the stairs when I came down." Her voice was brash but Giselle knew that she asked the question in earnest.

She replied with equal earnest, "If I didn't know better, I would say that he was thoughtful."

"Maybe he is? How could we know?" Edith declared. She sipped her coffee more slowly now. "Maybe he is," she repeated quietly. She looked up intently at Giselle. "He's been different everyone says, since Oscar died."

"Yes, he has," Giselle confirmed. "More reserved, if that's possible. But over the past few days I think he's begun with his hand gestures again. I would love to see that come back."

"Yes. Has to have been a shock to him, regardless. And not so much Oscar, but Lawrence going away like that. He was a first-class fool to confess. Everyone knows he wouldn't have it in him to do something like that. Still, I'd like to shake the hand of the person that really did," Edith proclaimed. "My brother was the worst kind of miserable snake." She didn't often let her feelings get the better of her, but Edith was nearing the end of her rope. "You know we have to get him out of there. Lawrence can't make it in prison. We have to find out who really did it."

Giselle felt her hand jerk involuntarily. Coffee slopped out of the cup onto the table. She quickly rose to get a towel. Edith caught a glimpse of her face before she turned away. It had contorted to fear. Had she done it? Was she fearful for herself? Or for someone else?

"How is that possible? To find a *keel-er! Mon Dieu!*" Giselle gulped as she returned to the table. Her accent had deepened. It happened when a person reverted back to their basic instincts, their core feelings. That fact was not lost on Edith. "The police consider the case closed," Giselle quavered.

"They do. I don't." Edith growled. "I've had enough. The boy needs his father." She drained her coffee, stomped over to the counter and clattered the cup down next to the sink.

"What will you do?" Giselle countered with a worried voice.

Edith paused. She toyed with the ever-present pearls around her neck. "Don't know. Don't know yet. I'll think of something." Then she marched from the room.

Giselle looked back at the window. The rain was still pouring down, but its invisible protective wall that she had always felt was gone.

૏

"Where's the money?"

Johnson looked up from the report that he held at arms length in front of him, in spite of his reading glasses, and squinted at his partner. "Huh? Whaddya mean?"

"I mean, who inherited? Who got Oscar Bernstein's money? And where is it? Invested?" Nick asked.

Johnson dropped the report on the desk and started flipping through the file.

"I don't remember anything about money. He was rich for sure, but the whole thing wasn't about that. It seemed to focus on the kid. Did he or didn't he do it, could he even stand trial…" Nick rambled.

"Ah, here it is!" Johnson was ignoring his partner. "Copy of the will, or the juicy parts anyway. Hmm," he trailed off as he read.

"Care to share it?" Nick asked after several moments.

Johnson glanced at him. "Oh. Yeah. Says that the son got half of it. Other half went to the sister, Edith. Except for this part, which is interesting. He gave a hundred grand to that housekeeper, but if she took it, he would have *'a letter in the hands of my attorneys delivered to my son immediately.'* If she declined the money, the letter would be *'retained by the attorneys for a period of one year, then destroyed'.*"

"That's weird," Nick remarked.

"Very weird. Can he make a condition like that?" Johnson asked.

Nick was thinking back to his law-school days. He came from a family of lawyers and had earned his Juris Doctorate but never pursued the career. He'd only studied law to appease his family. Nick had put in many hours hovering over books filled with cases. He tried to remember if anything he'd encountered would shed light on such a strange bequest. "From what I remember in law school, there are only three conditions placed on a bequest that aren't allowed: marriage, divorce, or a change of religion."

"So you can't leave a million bucks to someone only if they divorce their spouse, for example," Johnson said.

"Correct. But conditions are tricky because who's really going to enforce them? In this case, though, the lawyers would probably be paid from his estate for the year that they held the letter. If they held it. Does the file say if the housekeeper… what was her name?"

Johnson shuffled through the file again. "Giselle. Giselle Guerrette."

"Does it say if Ms. Guerrette took the money?" Nick continued.

Johnson looked through the papers once again and shook his head. "Nope. Doesn't say."

"Huh. Gimme that. I might be able to give that law firm a call," Nick said, catching the file as Johnson slid it across the desk toward him. "Let's see…" he found the name of Oscar Bernstein's attorney then looked up the number and pulled out his cell phone. Johnson eased his large bulk back into the decrepit metal swivel chair and laced his fingers together over his belly. He looked down at it and sighed. The diet hadn't been working as quickly as he'd hoped. He reached down to his waist and pulled the pedometer off his belt, looked at it, and swore softly. He leaned forward, stood with a groan, replaced the pedometer and began walking in circles around the desk.

Nick was now talking with the lawyer. He looked up at Johnson and mouthed, "Do you mind?" Johnson just pointed to his pedometer and kept walking. When Nick got off the phone he said, "Okay, that's annoying. You need to sit." Johnson complied, and Nick continued. "Bottom line, she didn't take the money, and they still have the letter."

Johnson stood and started circling again, although this time with a brighter expression. "Now *that's* interesting!" he remarked. "What could make a housekeeper turn down a big sum of money like that? Must be some big secret, eh?" He continued pacing.

"Okay, you have to stop. You're making me dizzy," Nick said. "We can't speculate on what's in the letter. Could be anything, but it has to be some kind of dirt on the housekeeper that she wouldn't want Lawrence Bellamy to find out about."

"I'd call that a loose end that needs to be tied up," Johnson said. "I knew there was more to this case. It was closed way too fast after Bellamy confessed."

"I agree," Nick responded. "Are you thinking what I'm thinking?"

"That I could use a cup of coffee and about six cinnamon bear claws?" Johnson muttered.

Nick chuckled. "Sorry on the bear claws, but I can do the coffee. C'mon. You can get more steps counted on that thing."

Johnson slung on his jacket and followed Nick out the door.

☙

Dulcie closed her laptop. "Done!" she announced out loud to the empty room. She had been emailing and coordinating details for the Outsider Art exhibit all morning and felt exhausted. "How about a walk. Fresh air, that's what I need," she murmured, more quietly this time.

"Back in a while – just a quick walk!" she called out to Rachel as she passed her desk. "Need anything?"

"Nothing you could get on a quick walk, or even a long one for that matter. But thanks for offering," Rachel quipped without looking up.

Dulcie laughed as she stepped out into the chilly fall air, and quickly reached into her pocket for her leather gloves. One fell on the brick sidewalk and she leaned down to pick it up. As she straightened, she found herself gazing across the street at Nicholas Black and Adam Johnson. She felt her heart thud, just once. Odd. She thought she'd been able to get over any ridiculous sort of crush she might have had on the detective.

Both men looked over at the same time as if reading her thoughts. Dulcie felt herself blush and was glad that they were all the way across the street. They stepped off the sidewalk and crossed over to her.

"Before you make any accusations, I just want you to know that I have not been doing any sort of private investigating on my own," Dulcie said as soon as they were within earshot. She looked down at her hands as she pulled on her gloves, hoping her cheeks had returned to a normal color. "I've been crazy busy with the new exhibit," she added.

"We wouldn't make any accusation of the kind," Nick reassured.

"Yes, we would," Johnson corrected. Nick shot him a menacing look. "We're getting coffee. Wanna join us?" Johnson asked, changing the subject.

"I would. Thanks," Dulcie answered. "I just came out to clear my head."

"Mind if we fill it up again with the latest puzzle?" asked Nick.

"Nope. Go right ahead," she replied.

"First of all, we can discuss this whole Oscar Bernstein case pretty openly since it's already been closed," Nick said. "So tell us what you think of this. Oscar Bernstein left $100,000 to his housekeeper, but if she took it, a certain letter would be delivered to Lawrence Bellamy."

Dulcie's forehead wrinkled. "That's strange," she commented. "So, did she take it?"

"She did not," Johnson replied.

"Well it begs the question: what's in the letter? Does anyone know where it is?" Dulcie asked.

"Yes. It's with his lawyer. Oscar's lawyer."

"Now I'll ask the obvious question: has anyone read it yet?" Dulcie wondered.

Johnson and Nick exchanged glances. "No, not yet," Nick said. "We just learned about it. But we were speculating on what Oscar Bernstein might have known about his housekeeper that would cause her to turn down that kind of money. What could he have written to Lawrence Bellamy?"

"Who said it was something that Oscar wrote?" Dulcie asked. "Maybe it was a letter that she had written to someone and Oscar had managed to get hold of it, or maybe someone else wrote a letter implicating someone for something."

Johnson nodded. "Good point. But we can't exactly march in to the lawyer's office and demand to read it. This is where the case being closed works against us. We have no reason to ask for it. We certainly couldn't get any kind of search warrant."

As they entered the coffee shop a man at the counter turned around holding a steaming mug. He looked at Dulcie and smiled. It was a slightly intimate smile. Nick recognized him instantly. It was the man he had seen Dulcie with before.

"Dulcie!" he exclaimed. "What a pleasure. I was just thinking about you!"

'*I'm sure you were,*' Nick thought.

"Raymond," Dulcie replied trying to keep her voice in a businesslike tone. "I'm glad to run into you. I've just put together the details this morning of filming Xander. I'll send you all of the information."

"Wonderful! I'm looking forward to our little project," he said. As he did he looked at the other two men curiously. They were obviously with Dulcie.

"Oh, let me introduce my friends," Dulcie said quickly. Nick felt himself cringing at the word *friend*. "These are Detectives Nicholas Black and Adam Johnson of the Portland Police."

They shook hands as Raymond annoyingly teased, "Dulcie, I hope you aren't in some kind of trouble!"

Nick stepped forward. "Not at all. Dulcie has worked with us before on some cases involving artworks. Her insight has been invaluable," he added.

Now Raymond remembered him. The man he had seen on the street looking at Dulcie through the window. '*Interesting,*' thought Raymond. '*Clearly he's carrying a torch. The question is, does Dulcie also?*'

Dulcie turned to Nick and Johnson. "This is Dr. Raymond Armand. He's the psychologist who has worked with Xander Bellamy. I'm putting together a mini-documentary on Xander for the new exhibit, and Raymond has been kind enough to help."

'*I'll bet he has,*' thought Nick.

"You see," Raymond interjected, "Xander is such a unique case and with my opportunity to work with him at length as a psychologist, I can provide the greatest access to fully understanding the way his mind works. Well," he chuckled in his ever-present self-deprecating manner, "As much as anyone can really know how his mind works."

Johnson stared at him for a moment, then cleared his throat. "That's great. Excuse me, I'll get us coffee," he muttered to Nick as he moved quickly toward the counter. "To go," he added over his shoulder, remembering that Raymond would obviously be finding a table.

Nick blinked several times. He hadn't anticipated such a level of arrogance from someone that Dulcie seemed to know so well. "Are you currently his doctor?" he asked.

"No, not at this point. The family feels that he is doing fine now after my extensive work with him. I'm very happy to consult on Dulcie's project," he touched Dulcie's arm for a moment, "and to see Xander again. He has such a wonderful talent."

Nick did not like Dr. Raymond Armand. Nick had always trusted his instincts, relying heavily on first impressions. As a detective it was a crucial part of his work. The first time he had seen Dr. Armand, through the window at this very coffee shop, he had not liked him. Did Dulcie? Nick glanced over at her.

She quickly spoke. "Xander is amazing. I'm looking forward to seeing him again. Ah, here's Adam with our coffee," she quickly took the cup that he handed her. "I must get back to the museum. Did you gentlemen have any other questions for me? I'd be happy to walk back with you," she said.

Nick knew exactly what she was doing. "Yes, I have another matter I'd like to get your opinion on." He turned to Raymond and shook his hand briefly. "Good to meet you," he said, then turned away. Johnson grunted the same to Raymond and headed for the door.

"As I said, I'll send you the information on the shoot," Dulcie repeated to Raymond. He smiled cloyingly in reply.

They were no more than twenty feet from the door when Nick blurted out, "Doctor? He considers himself a doctor?"

Dulcie didn't like Dr. Raymond Armand, but she also did not appreciate Nick's manner. "He is a doctor," she contended.

"Not in that sense!" Nick replied. "Not a medical doctor. He's not a psychiatrist, right? He's a psychologist."

"And earning a doctorate isn't difficult? Is that what you're implying?" Dulcie knew exactly what he meant. Why was she arguing this point?

"That's not at all what I mean. You have a doctorate. I know it takes a huge amount of work, not to mention dedicating a chunk of your lifetime. It's just that he seems to pass himself off as something that he's not," Nick trailed off.

"I disagree," Dulcie argued. The conversation paused for several moments.

Finally, Nick broke the silence. "I've got some things to do back at the station. You heading back?" he asked Johnson pointedly.

"Yeah, but I need to walk a little more," he pointed to the pedometer on his belt. "You head back. I'll see the lady back to her door, then meet you at the office."

"Good," Nick replied. "Good to see you again, Dulcie," he added somewhat stiffly. She smiled quickly at him but turned away.

As she continued with Johnson up the street he said, "You know exactly what he meant."

She sighed. "Yes, I do," she admitted.

"And don't forget, he went to law school. He has a doctorate, too."

Dulcie had forgotten. Now she felt foolish. It had been a stupid point to argue, especially since she basically agreed with Nick. Raymond did try to cast himself as something more than he was. It was annoying.

"You ever gonna forgive him?" Johnson asked quietly.

Dulcie was thoughtful as they walked along. "I know it's been quite a while now, but I felt like a fool. I felt like he betrayed me," Johnson started to speak but she cut him off. "I know, I know! He didn't. Not really. But it just felt like that." She knew that she sounded like a silly teenager.

"Maybe you could just start over," Johnson suggested. For all his gruff manner, he had a fatherly side that he could adopt when required.

Dulcie nodded. They reached the front door of the museum, and Johnson opened it for her. "Just think about it," he said. "Nick has his heart in the right place. He's a good person. Not many like him these days. 'Cept me, of course."

Now Dulcie laughed. "Thank you, Adam. I needed to hear that about Nick. You're right. I'll try – to start over, that is. And thanks for the coffee."

"Any time," he replied and closed the door behind her.

Adam Johnson returned to the police station. "Just gave her a talkin' to. Reminded her you've got a doctorate, too."

Nick looked up from his computer. "Johnson! Look, don't…"

Johnson raised his beefy hand to stop Nick's rapidly increasing volume. "You've been through hell and back already. Not sayin' it wasn't partly your fault, but the past is the past. Can't change it, can't go back. Only thing that counts is today. Besides, I'm not allowed to put in a good word for my buddy? You need all the help you can get."

Nick shook his head trying, unsuccessfully, to hide a smile. Maybe Johnson was right. Maybe he did need some help. But right now, he wanted to focus. Something was niggling him about the Oscar Bernstein case. "You know, I'd like to meet this incarcerated gentleman. Seems that everyone speaks highly of him, and everyone thinks he's lying. I want to see what he's like."

Johnson attempted to look at his watch. He moved his arm straight out as far as he could and squinted at it. "Dammit. I need a bigger watch," he swore under his breath.

"It's four o'clock. What you need are better reading glasses," said Nick.

"I need no such thing! My eyes are fine. Not gettin' any worse, I'm sure," Johnson protested.

"Yeah, and I'm the Pope," muttered Nick. "Is it still visiting hours at the jail?"

"Yep" Johnson chirped.

"Wanna take a field trip?" Nick asked, closing his laptop and standing up.

"Sure! Should be fun!"

Nick shot Johnson a look that indicated he felt his partner had an odd definition of fun. They wove their way around the desks and out to Nick's car.

Nick drove. He always drove. Generally it took Johnson a good five minutes to clear out things from the front seat of his car. It was never messy or dirty, just cluttered with a constantly revolving mass of papers, junk mail, and empty coffee cups. As they reached the building and got out of the car, Johnson said, "Wait a second. Why are we seeing him?"

"Do we need a reason?" asked Nick.

"Well, it seems kinda weird to just show up. And the boss won't like it if it seems as though we're questioning him. Case is closed, remember?"

"Good point. How about this." Nick cleared his throat, "His son will participate in a museum exhibit which will contain video of him working. The museum director felt she needed to get the father's permission even though his Aunt is now a legal guardian. However, Dr. Chambers didn't feel comfortable coming to the prison, so she asked if we could on her behalf," Nick concluded.

"Dang. That's why you got that big fancy education, right? Makes you an awesome liar!"

"I only use it for good, not for evil," Nick said as they went through the door.

Soon, they were seated at a table in an otherwise empty room. An armed prison guard stood just outside the door. "What exactly are you gonna ask him?" Johnson whispered.

"First off, I'll say what I just told you outside, in case someone," Nick nodded his head in the guard's direction, "decides to chat about it. Then I want to ask him about his home life, before he came to this lovely place. I might try to push him a little, so follow my lead."

"So you're the bad cop and I'm the good cop now?" Johnson quipped.

Nick snorted. "Yeah, something like that."

They heard footsteps in the hallway, and the door opened.

Both detectives looked at Lawrence Bellamy and gawked. The man was enormous. He stood over six and a half feet tall and looked like he had hands the size of a tennis racket. Strangely, he wasn't lanky. He looked as though someone had simply taking a normal sized person and pressed the *enlarge* button.

The huge man sat gently in a chair opposite them. The guard who had led him in stationed himself inside the door. He looked alert yet bored.

"Mr. Bellamy, I'm Detective Nick Black, and this is my partner, Detective Adam Johnson. We just have some questions for you, but they don't pertain to the, uh, the reason why you're here."

Lawrence Bellamy nodded almost imperceptibly.

"The director of the Maine Museum of Art would like to work with your son on an exhibit she's putting together. She wanted your permission, but was," Nick hesitated, appearing to search for the right word, "Uncomfortable coming here herself."

Lawrence smiled slightly. "I'm with her," he said quietly.

Nick explained the project as briefly as possible to Xander's father. "So, is this something that you could approve for your son?" he concluded.

Lawrence nodded. "My son is very talented. He is limited in some ways, but has more capacity for understanding in other ways than anyone can possibly realize." His eyes glowed warmly as he spoke. "You have to get to know him, spend time with him, to identify with him, although some people could spend a lifetime with him and never appreciate how special he is."

Nick was surprised to hear this speech. He was surprised by Lawrence's voice, too. It was soft and low. It didn't fit with his body.

"Did everyone at home appreciate him?" asked Nick in an offhand manner.

Lawrence's eyes flashed. "Not everyone," he answered simply.

"Is that why you're here?" Nick coaxed.

Lawrence sat back in his chair and folded his arms. "I'm done talking about that. I've said everything I need to say."

Johnson leaned forward. "I don't think that's what he was asking," he said to Lawrence. "What Detective Black means is, did everyone in your household accept Xander for who he was? Did he have the support of everyone?"

"These are strange questions. You came here to get my permission. You got it."

Nick sighed. "Okay, Lawrence, you're right. They are strange, and I can't, or won't, explain why. Can you just answer anyway? Things certainly couldn't get worse for you and who knows, maybe we can help."

Lawrence shook his head. "You can't. I confessed. Besides, why would you want to help?"

"Just work with me?" Nick tried to keep himself from showing his frustration.

Lawrence stared at the table for a very long time. Nick held his breath. Johnson began fantasizing about a cinnamon roll. Both men were jarred when Lawrence at last broke the silence. His voice cut through the stagnant air.

"Oscar hated everyone. He enjoyed psychological games, twisting people's minds. He liked to make people afraid."

"Afraid of what?" asked Johnson.

"Anything. Whatever their greatest fear was, he would use it against them. He liked to watch them suffer." Lawrence's face tightened. His body seemed to shrink as he spoke. "The only person that he couldn't control was Xander. He couldn't reach Xander's mind and it made him more and more angry." Lawrence inhaled heavily. "Or so everyone thought. You see," he glanced at the guard who still looked bored. "I found a sketchbook," he said quietly. "In Xander's room. When I looked at the sketches... I can't explain this very well... they showed fear. The faces of people around him, but looking scared. I knew then that Xander was afraid, too."

"And you couldn't allow that," Johnson broke in.

Lawrence shook his head. "No. Oscar had already killed my wife, drove her to her death. I wouldn't let him hurt my son."

"So that's why you pushed him," Nick said.

"Yes," Lawrence replied softly.

"Lawrence, tell me. Did any discussion of this sketchbook come out in your trial? Or did you simply stick to the events that allegedly happened?" Nick was careful to use the word *allegedly*. He wanted to see how Lawrence would react.

"It's how they did happen," Lawrence blurted. "We argued and I pushed him. That's all. No, there was no discussion about the sketchbook. No one asked for details when I confessed."

Nick and Johnson exchanged glances. Nick looked back at Lawrence. "Thank you for talking with us. Thank you for your honesty." He saw Lawrence's eyes flutter as he heard that last word while rising from his chair. "And thanks for giving permission to the museum to work with Xander." Nick held out his hand. Lawrence's nearly enveloped it, but the handshake was soft. Gentle.

What moves men of genius,
or rather what inspires their work,
is not new ideas,
but their obsession with the idea
that what has already been said
is still not enough.
~ Eugene Delacroix

CHAPTER EIGHT

The next morning, Dulcie paced her office floor in front of Detective Nicholas Black. She stopped and whirled around to face him. "Now let me get this straight. You think Lawrence Bellamy is innocent. But you need proof. So you want me to smuggle you and Adam Johnson in as part of the film crew so that you can have access to the house to search Xander's room, without a warrant, I might add, and find a sketchbook."

"That sums it up," Nick stated.

Dulcie leaned against her desk looking thoughtful. Her dark brown hair was pulled softly into a low chignon, and several wisps had escaped already. She reached up and attempted to slide them back in, but they simply fell forward again. Nick was glad. They made her look angelic, he thought.

"If I didn't agree with you about Lawrence Bellamy, I'd say absolutely not. But I do agree with you. We have one problem, though," she explained. "Raymond Armand will be there. He knows you and Adam. He'll wonder what you're doing. I'll have to tell him."

'*Damn*,' thought Nick. This *Dr. Armand* was turning out to be trouble in more ways than one. Then he noticed that Dulcie had not used the title 'Doctor' before his name. Was that on purpose? Was she remembering their previous argument? Nick decided to let it go. *Least said, soonest mended* was the phrase he remembered hearing as a boy.

"How do you think Armand would respond?" Nick asked. "We'll be stealing, technically, if we take the sketchbook."

"Who says you're taking it? You could simply be borrowing it, and you'll bring it back. Besides, Raymond doesn't need to know about the sketchbook. We could say that you're investigating someone else in the crew and needed to get the inside scoop."

"You really should have been a detective," Nick marveled. "You know how to lie without lying."

"Nick! That's terrible!" Dulcie swatted him playfully on the arm. His heart made a single, huge thump in his chest. He was sure she could have heard it. He tried to refocus. She was still speaking. "I don't think we'll have any trouble with him, though. He'll be too busy trying to sound overtly intellectual. Serious ego we're contending with there."

Nick felt his entire body relax. So, she really didn't like Dr. Raymond Armand. That competition was out. Good. He brought his thoughts back to the discussion. "You'll have the most difficult job, pretending that you don't know us."

"Maybe, but I'll be pretty busy, too. I won't need to interact much with you. The question now is, do we tell the film crew, or just let them assume that you are two other 'helpers' that we brought in?"

"See, this is what I'm talking about. You're really good at this!" Nick grinned.

"Fine. I now have a Plan B if this art career doesn't work out," she laughed. "Now be off with you! Some of us have work to do!"

"All right. See you tomorrow afternoon at Xander's house. One o'clock," Nick replied.

"Perfect," Dulcie said, already typing on her laptop. "See you tomorrow."

છ

It didn't sit well. Edith Bernstein did not like it when life was untidy. The situation with Xander's father was definitely not tidy. She was stooped over, tying on her "walking shoes" as she called them. They were actually brown leather sneakers, "tennis shoes" according to the box, but she had always believed she would never purchase any athletic wear, so they were her walking shoes. She didn't consider walking athletic. She considered it a necessity.

From the house, two pathways led to the beach. One was direct, but the other twisted and turned through the pine trees and underbrush. Edith preferred that one. At a steady pace, it took a good fifteen minutes to reach the water, then another fifteen back. Half an hour was a good amount of time to think something through.

She set off at a slowish pace, hands clasped behind her. It was her thinking gait.

'*So, let's begin,*' she thought. '*Gisa meets Lawrence Bellamy, Canadian from Quebec. They have Xander and quickly know something is wrong. Oscar takes them in. Gisa's mother has already died. Gisa begins drinking heavily and taking sleeping pills. Giselle has been hired long before to help out.*'

Dulcie stopped. When exactly had Giselle come into the picture? What did anyone know about her? It was common knowledge that she had come in to clean their house in Quebec when Lawrence and Gisa had lived there. She had been in America with them for several years now and had practically raised Xander. Edith set these thoughts aside, to be continued later. She was very good at bookmarking her thoughts and returning to them. It was methodical.

She started walking again. '*Oscar pays for Xander's therapy. He pays for everyone's expenses while they live in the house. Xander's condition improves, but his mother's deteriorates. She dies of an overdose of sleeping pills mixed with alcohol. No one knows if it was intentional or not. Oscar becomes more intense with his mind games.*'

Edith could see how Lawrence would be pushed too far. She could certainly sympathize with him. He was always a quiet, good man. He had wanted to help his wife and his child. In the end, he could only help one of them. Edith could see how anyone would be driven, under those circumstances, to push someone through a window during a heated argument. She just couldn't see Lawrence actually doing it. He had always been aware of his size. He had always been careful with everyone around him, almost to the point of being overly polite and self-conscious. Still....

Her thoughts switched to others who had been around at that time, and rested on Raymond Armand. *'That psychologist needs his comeuppance. He knows his stuff, but he really thinks too highly of himself.'* Edith slowed her pace. Could he have been involved? He was in the house quite often. Giselle had told her that he was angry when Oscar had discontinued his services. Evidently he wanted to make a name for himself using Xander as his research guinea pig. Everyone believed that Oscar removed Raymond Armand from the household because he didn't want the world to know about Xander. Was that the only reason? Would that have been enough to make Raymond want to push Oscar out of a window? Was Raymond the shadow in Xander's painting?

Edith had reached the beach. She stopped and gazed out across the ocean. She had crossed that water so many times in her travels. It looked peaceful today, barely rippling. Tomorrow it could be different. Tomorrow huge waves could roll in from some distant storm that would never even make landfall. One large event, setting off a chain reaction that would continue rolling on for hundreds of miles and perhaps several days.

One event. A chain reaction. Was that the key? Why had her mind thought of that? Edith did not believe in random thoughts, not in her own brain anyway. Everything that popped into her head was there for a reason. She stored away this particular thought, bookmarking it to return to later when it seemed more relevant. And it would be relevant, in some way. She was sure of it.

☙

Giselle scurried around the house picking up various breakable items and temporarily storing them in a small back room which she intended to lock. Even though Dulcie had said that the film crew would be in Xander's studio only, she imagined them traipsing through the entire house with big, heavy equipment, knocking over anything and everything in their path. As she made one final sweep through, she picked up a few more things that weren't breakable, but certainly had a great deal of value: an antique wooden globe, a first edition novel…. *'No sense in tempting fate,'* she thought.

She continued upstairs and forced herself to go in to Oscar Bernstein's old study. She hated that room. She had always made sure that he was nowhere in the house when the room needed cleaning. Even with him gone, she still felt uneasy every time she was in the room.

Giselle remembered the last argument very well. She had witnessed all of it. Oscar had summoned her and Lawrence. He had told Lawrence that he would no longer be paying for Dr. Raymond Armand's services, and that the man was no longer welcome in the house. Lawrence had been furious, in his own quiet way. The psychologist had done well with Xander; Xander had been using hand signals more. But Oscar had found a way to kill two birds with one stone. He had simultaneously squashed Dr. Armand's intention to make his work with Xander public, and he had struck at where Lawrence was most vulnerable. Giselle remembered how Oscar had simply sneered at Lawrence, telling him to shut up or he and his "worthless spawn" would be living on the street. Then Oscar had laughed that disgusting, maniacal snicker. It had been horrifying.

Giselle had not known why she had been summoned also. Perhaps simply as a witness to this announcement, to add to Lawrence's distress? No, Oscar was always one step ahead of everyone. He told Giselle to stay as Lawrence stormed out. She did so, but edged toward the door.

When Lawrence was out of earshot, Oscar had said, "My dear little Giselle. You have some secrets, don't you." His voice was slippery and menacing. She did have secrets. What could he know? She did not reply. "You see, I know everything. I always know everything!" He laughed again. "Let me see, one of them involves the good Dr. Armand, doesn't it? You certainly have reason to want him to continue his work with Xander, don't you?"

Giselle stood as firmly as she could, willing her body not to shake. She did not reply.

"You and the good doctor certainly got along well!" Oscar was now ogling her, his eyes scanning up and down her body. He rubbed his hands together. "Such a pity he won't be around to see to your needs. You'll have to find solace elsewhere!" He began to walk toward her. The next thing that she remembered was bolting down the stairs, nearly tripping on the carpet, then throwing herself in her room and locking the door. She could still hear his horrible laugh ringing in the hallway.

"What else could he know?" she whispered to the empty room. Everything else was so far buried in the past, she couldn't imagine how he could manage to dig it up. After the will reading, when she had refused the money for fear of that letter being sent to Lawrence, she had asked if she could read it. The attorneys had refused stating client confidentiality. She didn't understand how that could apply if the client was dead. They had rambled on with something about the client now being the estate, which she still did not understand. She really didn't care about the money. She just didn't want certain information to surface. It might not change anything, but then again, it could bring her whole world crashing down. Giselle shook her head rapidly, trying to rid herself of unwelcome thoughts. She glanced around the room, then retreated quickly.

She continued into Xander's bedroom. She had seen him working in his studio, as always. She would have to take him for a walk later. He needed some fresh air. As she straightened things up, something dropped to the floor from the windowsill, behind the curtains. It was a sketchbook. Giselle picked it up and flipped it open.

Then she recalled the conversation she had had with Lawrence. She visited him at least once each week to give him news about Xander. She worried about him in prison, away from his son. It wasn't right. Yesterday, he had told her that two detectives had come to see him. They asked questions about Xander and Oscar. He had told them about the sketchbook. Giselle had not known about it.

She looked at the pages filled with black and white sketches. Lawrence was right. Fear. People's faces, even their bodies, were contorted in fear. It made her feel sick to think that Xander could have felt this fear also. To be able to capture the emotion with such raw intensity, how could he not feel it as well? Fear was one of the most basic, primal emotions, after all. Of any emotion, why wouldn't fear be an obvious one for Xander to know?

The book had been kept hidden for a reason. She was sure of that. Xander had never painted pictures like these in his studio. He must have realized, somehow, that he could not let anyone know that he understood, that he might also feel afraid.

Giselle continued turning page after page. At last she flipped to the last one and gasped. It showed Oscar, lying on the ground by the house. Above him was a broken window. The dark pool around his head seemed to flow and increase in size as Giselle stared at the page. Yet this was not what surprised her. What had made her gasp was the image of a man, crouched on the ground beside Oscar. The man was Lawrence.

Giselle remembered. The sound of glass breaking. The horrible scream. As she stared at the drawing, a thought slowly began to form in her head. She looked up and gazed out the window, seeing nothing.

It might work. It just might work. It could be exactly what was needed to get Lawrence out of prison.

೮೮

Dulcie had arranged to visit Xander's home late in the afternoon on the day before the video shoot. She heard the gravel crunch in the driveway under the tires of her battered Jeep Wrangler. She'd thought of getting a new car so many times, but in the end couldn't part with what she considered her baby. They had been through too much together.

She parked, grabbed her leather briefcase, now soft and worn after having seen nearly as many years as the vehicle, and strode to the door. Before she even rang the bell, Edith swung the door wide.

"Good. Punctual. I like that."

Dulcie bit her lip to stop from grinning. "Yes, Mrs. Bernstein. I like that, too. I think it's rude to keep people waiting."

"Exactly!" said the imposing woman. She stepped back to let Dulcie through.

"I just wanted to review everything with you and Giselle for tomorrow.

"Good. Come in here," Edith said and headed for the same room that Dulcie had been in before with Edith for tea.

Dulcie hesitated. "Would Xander join us in here?"

Edith stopped short, swiveled around and shot a piercing look at Dulcie. "Why?" she barked.

Dulcie took a large gulp of air and said calmly, "Because all of this pertains to him. It disrupts his work and is intrusive. He should at least be present when we go through what will happen tomorrow."

The piercing look continued, then Edith shrugged her shoulders. "Fine. Doubt he'll get a thing out of it, but that's fine. He's in the kitchen with Giselle. We can talk there." She led the way.

Dulcie was relieved to be in the far less formal setting of the kitchen. Giselle and Xander sat at the table, each with a cup of tea. Giselle stood immediately and said warmly, "Ah, Dul-cee. So good to see you! I will get you tea. And you as well," she nodded in Edith's direction.

"Thank you, Giselle. That would be lovely," Dulcie replied. She and Edith sat at the table with Xander. He had not acknowledged them in any way. He simply continued to drink his tea and occasionally take a bite of what appeared to be a blueberry scone.

"Don't wait for me, Dulcie. You begin. I can hear you from here," Giselle said over her shoulder.

Dulcie pulled a notebook from her bag. "All right. I've tried to design the schedule so that we intrude as little as possible. I've instructed everyone to arrive at nine o'clock exactly and not a moment later. I've also told them that they cannot enter the house until then either. I know that Xander typically begins shortly after nine. The crew will come in quickly and quietly, set up in his studio, and begin filming."

"What will you film first?" asked Giselle, now joining them at the table with a tray. She passed a steaming cup to Dulcie while Edith helped herself.

"First we'll just get various details of the room to piece in as background. The easel, Xander's paints, the view from his window… then we'll bring in the model."

"Who's that?" Edith queried. "Hope it's not some out-of-work actor."

Dulcie laughed. "No, far from it. We have someone that I know well, but who isn't a model or an actor. We wanted to make sure that it was someone Xander had never seen before."

Edith snorted. "Sounds like an out-of-work actor to me."

"You might say he's between gigs," Dulcie quipped. "But he certainly isn't an actor. He runs a touring company and takes people on excursions in the bay on his yacht. However, this is the time of year when business really begins to slow down, as you can imagine. He's happy to have some extra work." Dulcie did not mention that he also happened to be her brother.

Edith harrumphed an incomprehensible response.

Dulcie turned to Xander. "You do not need to participate at all if you don't like this," she said directly to him. "Just stay in your room, or leave at any time. I want you to be comfortable with what we're doing."

"Boy doesn't know what you're saying," Edith blurted mid-sip. "Only understands direct actions. Walk. Eat. Paint."

Dulcie ignored Edith's comment and sat very still as she looked at Xander. She felt as though she was watching a wild bird, hoping that it would slowly hop toward her.

Xander put down his cup but continued to stare into it. His hand moved to the table. Then he flipped the hand over so that it rested palm up. Dulcie looked up at Giselle. Her eyes were wide. She glanced back at Dulcie and nodded. *Yes*, Dulcie could hear her thinking, *he has just spoken to you.*

"Thank you," Dulcie said quietly to Xander. He continued to stare into his teacup.

She continued to relate more details of the next day to them, but half of her thoughts were still on Xander. He had communicated. Again. What else could be happening in his mind?

Dulcie finished discussing the details. Xander had already left the room.

"So you'll be done by three o'clock at the latest?" declared Edith.

"Yes, and if all goes well, sooner," Dulcie said.

"Good. That's it then. Thank you for coming by," Edith stood and marched out.

Giselle and Dulcie looked at each other. Both spontaneously giggled.

"She is always like that. You must excuse her," Giselle said. "She has a good heart, though."

"I can see that," Dulcie agreed. "And she obviously cares a great deal about Xander. In her way."

"Yes, *in her way*. That is a kind way to say it," Giselle offered thoughtfully. "But *Dul-cee*, I must show you something. It is very odd. Can you wait here a moment?"

"Of course," Dulcie said.

Giselle left, and Dulcie heard her running quickly upstairs. After several moments, she returned to the kitchen with a wire-bound book in her hand. She gave it to Dulcie.

"What are your thoughts of this, as one who looks at art a great deal?"

Dulcie began looking through the drawings and immediately realized what it must be. This was the sketchbook that Nick had told her about. She considered each sketch more carefully now, hesitating over some. "These are Xander's, I assume," she said without looking up. "It's obvious from his style. What I find so difficult to understand about him is that he can capture the emotions of others so well, but he has none of his own." She was still turning the pages.

"Does he have none of his own?" Giselle asked, "Or does he simply show none of his own?"

"That's a good point," Dulcie acknowledged. She reached the last drawing and involuntarily sat back quickly in her chair. She forced herself to lean forward again. "Giselle, is this what I think it is?"

"Yes," Giselle breathed.

She could barely hear the other woman's voice. "Who is the man kneeling over him?" Dulcie asked.

"That is Lawrence, his father," Giselle whispered.

Dulcie continued to stare at the two men. Slowly, she began to realize the implication of the drawing. She looked up at Giselle. "Xander only draws what he sees," she said.

"Yes," Giselle repeated.

Dulcie looked up at the open, partially broken window on the second floor, the one that Oscar Bernstein had obviously just come hurtling through. In the background, there was a shadow. An unmistakable shadow.

"But Giselle, look," she pointed at it.

"Yes, I know. It is someone in the room," she said.

Dulcie sat back again. "What are you going to do with this?" she asked.

"I thought I would take it to the police? I know that Lawrence confessed, but this could prove it false, perhaps? I told the police that I was outside, walking with Xander. This proves that to be true. He could not have drawn this if he had not seen it."

"And that in turn proves that Xander could not have pushed his grandfather out the window. But I don't see how it helps Lawrence. Yes, there's a shadow of a person in Oscar's study. But Lawrence could have pushed Oscar, then run downstairs and outside to his body."

Giselle shook her head. "*Non, jamais!*" Her French edged its way in as she became agitated. "I followed Xander on the trail. We both heard glass breaking and a scream. We did not see him fall but we emerged from the trees immediately after. Lawrence would not have had enough time to leave Oscar's study, come down the stairs, proceed down the hall, and come out this door," she pointed to the picture, "in that amount of time. *Impossible!*" Her accent was pronounced again on the final word.

"So someone was up there," Dulcie said.

Giselle did not reply.

"Giselle, I know who should see this. I mean, I know who on the police force should see this. Could I keep it? Could I bring it to him?"

"By all means. If this helps Lawrence to come home to his son, then… by all means! We all know that he could not have done it!"

Dulcie carefully closed the sketchbook and put it in her briefcase. She thanked Giselle who now walked her to the door.

"*Non*, I must thank you," Giselle said. "Since you have come into our lives, I have sensed something different in this house."

"Me?" Dulcie proclaimed. "Something from me?"

"It is difficult to explain," Giselle replied. "But the only word I can think of is *espérance*. Hope." She smiled at Dulcie. "We shall see you tomorrow. Thank you, again," she added and gently closed the door.

Dulcie stood for several moments on the steps, looking bewildered.

"You'll never guess what I have!" As a rule, Dulcie did not talk on the phone while driving. She had just pulled into the museum parking lot. The car was still running. She tried to turn off the car with her left hand and nearly dropped the phone in the process.

Quickly switching hands with the phone she heard Nick say, "Want me to try, or would you rather just…"

She cut him off. "I have the sketchbook! And wait till you see it! It's a doozy!"

"A good doozy, or a bad doozy?" he asked.

"Shut up and get over here!" Dulcie exclaimed.

"Fine, but where is *here*?" Nick laughed.

"Oh, sorry. At my office. The museum. Oh, wait. If we're closed by the time you get here, just rap on the door. I'll tell the guard to let you in."

"Great. See you in ten minutes!" Nick turned to Johnson who was walking laps around the desks again.

"Looks like more walking for you! How many paces to the museum?"

"A lot!" Johnson said happily. "What's up?" he added, pausing briefly.

"Tell you on the way," Nick said throwing on his jacket.

"Okay, but slow down a little! I don't want this dammed thing to screw up the count and miss any!"

Nick just shook his head. By the time they reached the museum, Johnson knew what they were about to see. He had voluntarily increased his pace while Nick talked. "This could be good!" he said.

Nick tapped on the door and the guard opened it. They hurried to Dulcie's office.

"Come over here and sit," she said, pointing to a table. She sat between them and opened the sketchbook. "It's decidedly Xander's, of course, and all of the drawings show the people around him with various expressions of fear. And then we come to this," she turned to the last page.

Nick and Johnson both leaned forward in front of Dulcie. She pushed her chair back, stood, then circled to the other side of the table. The two men leaned in even closer, their heads nearly touching.

"Okay, that's Lawrence," muttered Johnson. "And that's gotta be Oscar," said Nick. "Looks like the pictures of the crime scene."

"There's another detail you haven't caught yet," Dulcie interrupted. They both looked up simultaneously, then down again like two puppies. Dulcie pointed.

"What is that? Looks like…"

"A shadow. Of somebody. In Oscar's study. Huh!" Johnson was the first to sit back. He rubbed his eyes, then stood and started pacing the room.

Dulcie gave Nick a quizzical look. "He's wearing a pedometer. It's a bet with his wife. Don't ask," he said under his breath.

Dulcie hid her smile but was quickly serious again. "There's more to the story. As you know, because you've heard it over and over, Xander only paints, or draws, what he sees. So he obviously saw this scene," she gestured toward the sketchbook. "But that doesn't necessarily mean anything. However, Xander was out walking with the housekeeper, Giselle. She said that they were returning to the house when they heard glass breaking, a scream, then within only a few seconds emerged from the woods to see this."

The two men stared at her blankly.

"Giselle also said that in the amount of time it took her to hear the glass break and the scream, then to come out of the trees and witness this," she pointed to the sketch, "Lawrence would never have been able to push Oscar out of the window, then run all the way down the stairs and through the house to get outside and reach the body. It isn't possible."

Nick nodded. "So, he must have been either outside or at least downstairs, near the door," he concluded.

"Right," said Dulcie. "And, this shadow in the window shows that there was someone else in that room!"

"Yeah, but here we go again," Johnson chided. "Xander gives us another shadow."

"True," Nick said. "But the fact that it's there. It's there in the painting and it's there in the sketch. We can't discount it." He raked his hand through his hair. "Besides, we don't have to necessarily prove who killed Oscar Bernstein. The first step could be to prove that Lawrence made a false confession, and that he *didn't* do it"

Johnson stopped. "Right. So, Mr. Law-degree, what's it take to do that?"

Nick thought for a moment. "I'd say, convincing evidence to the contrary, and a compelling reason to make the false confession in the first place."

"This looks pretty convincing to me. Xander's work is pretty much like taking a photograph. He doesn't exactly embellish," Dulcie informed them.

"True, and with Giselle's claim that he couldn't have made it down there in the amount of time given," added Nick, "along with the compelling reason of protecting his son from being locked up in an institution…"

"Yeah, plus, it was Butt-head Butler who ran the initial investigation," Johnson chimed in from across the room. He had begun walking again.

Nick smirked and glanced at Dulcie. "Excuse him, but that's the nickname around the station. Butler is known for making enemies and sticking with his initial conclusion, right or wrong. He's pretty close to retirement. I think the chief is just waiting him out."

"Why would they put him on an important case like this?" Dulcie asked.

"There was no one else, probably," Nick answered.

"You know, Nick," Johnson mused, "Come to think of it, Chief's gotta know we're looking into this by now. I've thought it was funny that he hasn't come down on us yet. Maybe there's a reason? Maybe he knows Butler botched it, and he wants us to open it up again?"

Nick swiveled around in his chair to look at his partner. "OK, you gotta stop pacing. You're driving me nuts! I do agree, though. We've been allowed to quietly stay on this case for a reason." He turned back to the table and closed the sketchbook. "Could I take this?" he asked Dulcie. "We might have to use it as evidence."

"Yes, although I don't know if Xander realizes that it's missing," Dulcie said.

"Does that matter?" Nick said. "Would he even notice?"

"Yes, I think he would. You saw those drawings. He notices far more than we realize." She thought for a moment. "What if you bring the book with you tomorrow, and I'll talk to Xander about it. I'll know if it's okay with him."

Nick wasn't exactly sure how she could know, but he didn't question her. She'd brought the book to them in the first place, and technically the case was still closed so they couldn't confiscate if for evidence. "All right. But you keep it for now. I'll get it tomorrow," he said. "If I can," he added.

"Fine," Dulcie answered. "But now gentlemen, I need to get home. Tomorrow will be a busy day," she said.

"Would you like an escort home?" Nick asked quietly.

Johnson heard him. Without thinking he said, "Yeah, we can walk you home! That'll give me a thousand or so more steps, at least!"

Nick glared at his partner pointedly, but Johnson missed it. He was heading for the door. "C'mon kids! Let's get rolling!" he said, plowing across the museum's marble floor.

Nick mouthed "Sorry!" to Dulcie.

She giggled and whispered, "Let's go or we'll never catch him!"

CHAPTER NINE

Dulcie was always amazed by the amount of work that went into professional photography, especially a professionally done video. She had asked for a minimal amount of equipment, but there were still lights, screens deflecting the lights, tripods, and quite a few cords. They had brought only one microphone, however.

Dr. Raymond Armand stood back, observing the crew as they set up. He commented on the lack of microphone, concerned as he would be providing the narration. "I doubt anyone will be able to hear me fully," he sniffed.

"That's just for today. What I'd like to have you do is just narrate with your own thoughts as we go. Just respond to what you see. We'll watch the footage later, then do the actual narration in a recording booth," she reassured him.

Raymond had forgotten that part. "Ah, yes. Of course." He had wanted everyone in the room to hear him, but that was irrelevant compared to the many that would hear him as they saw the video.

Dulcie continued, "For that reason, if there are other sounds in the room, just ignore them. Keep talking. I think it's important to get your first reaction, your first impression."

"Absolutely," Raymond agreed. He believed it was important for anyone to benefit from his first, second, and third impression.

Dulcie stepped away and surveyed the mild chaos. She caught Nick's eye and jerked her head slightly toward the doorway. They met out in the hallway. "I'm going to speak to Xander now," she said. He saw that she had the sketchbook. "He's in his room, but the door is open." Dulcie glanced down the hall. "Giselle said that we can go in."

Nick nodded, and they quietly went down the hall. When they reached Xander's room, Dulcie tapped on the doorframe. Xander was seated in the window, looking out across the treetops, toward the ocean. He did not move or turn to acknowledge them but Dulcie saw his hands unclasp.

They joined him at the window. "It's a beautiful day, Xander, isn't it. Thank you for letting us be in your studio. I would like to ask one more thing. Would you allow my friend," she gestured toward Nick, "to borrow this?" she put the sketchbook on the window seat beside Xander. "I think that he can use it to help your father. My friend might be able to bring him back."

Nick was amazed. It was the oddest thing he had ever seen. It appeared that Dulcie was speaking to a statue. Nick thought of the Statue of David, the boy who had slain the terrible Goliath. Nick had seen it once, years ago on a family trip to Italy. Michelangelo's statue looked so real that Nick thought it might speak. Now he waited for Xander to speak, but like the statue, he did not.

Dulcie waited too. She knew that Xander would respond in some way. After several moments he moved his hand toward the sketchbook, then slid it almost imperceptibly along the seat toward Dulcie. He clasped his hands again. He had not altered his gaze out the window since they had entered the room.

As she had before, Dulcie simply whispered, "Thank you," in reply. She gently took the sketchbook, and went back into the hallway. Nick trailed along behind her, looking back at Xander several times.

"Wow!" he said when they were in the hallway again. "How do you know he's going to do anything when you just wait?" he asked.

"I don't, but I have a pretty good idea. I can't explain it, but I feel as though I understand him somehow," she replied.

"You've spent your life studying artists and working with artists, so if anyone could understand one, it would be you," Nick complimented her. He noticed that her cheeks flushed slightly.

"That's a very nice thing to say," she smiled, and handed him the sketchbook. "Now put this in a safe place!"

"Will do!" Nick answered. He located Johnson back in Xander's studio, and Dulcie saw them speaking quietly, heads bowed toward each other.

Giselle entered and stood next to Dulcie. "Are you ready for him yet?" she questioned.

"Yes, I think so," Dulcie said. "His model is hiding in the study where Xander won't see him yet. Let me just make sure that the crew is all set, then we can get them."

Dulcie walked around the room speaking with each group. Raymond had already stationed himself in front of the microphone and looked very self-satisfied. His voice, his wisdom would be the primary thing that everyone heard.

The director spoke to the room. "Let's get this in one take, please, if we can!" He nodded to Dulcie.

"Okay, go get him!" Dulcie said to Giselle. Moments later, Xander entered the room. The cameras had already begun to roll. He went straight to his easel, picked up a brush, and began dabbing at his palette. Dulcie knew this was the way he always started his work. She heard Raymond's voice. She had asked him to be as quiet as possible, and fortunately, he had complied.

Dulcie nodded to an assistant at the doorway, and she brought Dan in. Dan winked at Dulcie as he walked by. He positioned himself in front of Xander. Xander looked up at him. Then, Xander glanced at

Dulcie. His head swiveled back to Dan. He looked down and continued to dab at his palette.

Dulcie motioned for Dan to leave. He joined her at the back of the room. Dulcie held her breath. There was no guarantee that Xander would paint Dan. She was nervous as well, because she did not understand why Xander had focused briefly on her as well.

"What's he doing?" Dan whispered.

"I don't know," Dulcie whispered back.

Raymond glanced over at Dulcie questioningly. She simply shrugged her shoulders and made a rolling motion with her hands for him to continue talking. *No problem there*, she thought.

Xander turned to the canvas and, as always started at the top. The hair, then eyebrows, then eyes, nose, lips… it was a perfect likeness of Dan. Dulcie watched in amazement, but was concerned as well. Xander had not centered Dan on the canvas as he had in all of his other portraits.

Her curiosity was quickly answered. Xander moved his brush to the top of the canvas again and began painting another person. Hair, eyebrows eyes… Dulcie saw an image of herself appearing. Everyone in the room gasped.

"What…?" Dan said. Dulcie suddenly began laughing. "He knows! Dan, he can see a resemblance between us! He knows you're my brother!" It was Xander's way of making a joke.

When he finished, he put down the brush, and walked to the window, his back to everyone in the room. The crew director glanced at Dulcie. "All set?" he mouthed.

She nodded. Giselle went over to Xander and spoke to him. Dulcie saw her make the *eat* motion with her hand. They crossed the room and as they passed by Dulcie, Giselle whispered, "Lunchtime!" Dulcie smiled. Giselle knew exactly what Xander needed. She had always been there for him.

Always been there. Dulcie's mind stuck on the thought. There was a bond, almost a maternal bond, between Giselle and Xander. Dulcie knew that a bond like this could easily form after people had lived together for years, especially when one of those people was a child. Why did this bond seem different?

Dulcie's thoughts were jarred by Edith. "Well *that's* done! Got what you needed, I see. Museum will like this," she announced. "Let me see it before you go public. Family has to approve." She did not wait for an answer. It wasn't a question. She turned and marched from the room.

"Brunhilda approves, I see," Nick said as he sidled up behind Dulcie.

Dulcie snorted in response but quickly regained her composure. "Yes, always an advantage to stay on Edith Bernstein's good side," she admitted. She looked over at Xander's work. The video crew were now taking close-up shots of it. "I wish he hadn't painted me as well, though."

"Yeah, why'd he do that?" Johnson asked, joining them.

"I think, and this is pure conjecture, but I believe it was his way of making a joke. No one said anything about Dan being my brother. Xander recognized it, so instead of just painting him, he painted both of us."

Nick looked thoughtful. "Wouldn't that mean that he's creating his own images, though? He's not just painting what he sees?"

Dulcie shook her head. "Not at all. Look at the painting. He shows us separately. And look at the collar of my blouse. He's painted me wearing exactly what I have on today."

Nick glanced at her collar, then saw a simple gold necklace around her throat that he hadn't noticed before. Yes, Xander had caught that as well.

"Hey Nick," Johnson said slowly. "Just thought of something. While we're here, want to do a little experiment?"

"What kind of experiment?"

"Want to see how long it takes to run out of Oscar's study, down the stairs, though the hall, and outside where Oscar ended up? With all of these guys here," he waved around the room, "we wouldn't be causing much more commotion."

"Johnson, sometimes you're way smarter than you look," Nick said. "We'll have to hurry before they start hauling things down. Think it would be okay?" he asked Dulcie.

"I think so. Giselle and Xander are in the kitchen. Who knows where Edith is, but I daresay you can outrun her. Go, but be quick!"

"We intend to!" Nick said as they hurried away.

In the hallway, Johnson said, "Look, pains me to admit it, but you're probably faster. I'll go outside where the body was. You stand in the window. When you're ready to run, wave at me. I'll start with the time." He pointed unnecessarily to the watch on his wrist.

"Good plan!" Nick hurried toward the study.

Johnson quickly went outside. He looked up at the window. Nick gave him a thumbs-up sign. Johnson returned it. Then Nick waved and disappeared.

Johnson watched the seconds tick by. Eleven, twelve, thirteen, fourteen... Nick ran up beside him. He was panting from the sprint. "Ooh, see you're in good shape!" Johnson jested.

"Shut up," Nick replied. "How long?"

"Seventeen. That's a pretty long time."

"Yup. The housekeeper said it only took them 'a few' seconds to come out of the trees. We can ask her, but I'd say that's a lot shorter than seventeen. Plus, you might be a tad faster than Lawrence Bellamy."

"Agreed," Nick said. "So Giselle is right. Lawrence couldn't have pushed Oscar out the window."

"Unless..." Johnson thought aloud.

Nick groaned. "What now!"

"Unless he did it earlier. Remember, the scream Giselle heard could have been Lawrence. He might have pushed him out the window earlier."

Nick thought for a moment. "Let's check something. Come with me." They went to his car. Nick unlocked it and pulled Xander's sketchbook from the back seat. He flipped it open to the last page. "Look. Right there," he pointed. "There isn't a lot a blood around his head. Remember the photos? There was quite a lot of blood around him. Head wounds really bleed a lot. But the sketch shows very little. So it must have just happened."

Johnson was quiet. "I still don't get how that kid can do this," he said.

"I don't either," Nick replied, "But Dulcie's right. It is just like having a photograph. We're lucky he can do this." He shut the book. "Or rather, if I'm not mistaken, Lawrence Bellamy is lucky."

ଓଃ

The news stories were brief. Lawrence Bellamy had been exonerated and released from prison. No one knew who had killed Oscar Bernstein, but it was not Lawrence Bellamy. He had only confessed when he thought his son was being considered as a suspect. A new case had been opened, and Nick and Johnson now had the unenviable task of investigating to see who the real killer was.

"Here's something that strikes me as odd," said Johnson as he and Nick walked down a busy Portland street. "Lawrence is back, he didn't do it, so a killer is obviously at large. But no one over there is the slightest bit concerned. I mean, wouldn't you be just a little bit nervous if these hazy shadows showed up in the kid's artwork, and some guy gets pushed out a window by person or persons unknown who is obviously still at large?"

"Yup," Nick said. "Then again, they'd been dealing with the hell of Oscar Bernstein, so maybe they're grateful to this person or person's unknown. They don't see him, or her for that matter, as a threat."

"True. Good point. Maybe they don't care." He stopped, which was unusual for Johnson lately. He at least tried to march in place now when he wasn't walking. "They don't care or…"

Nick read his mind. "Or they know who did do it."

"Exactly," Johnson agreed. "In which case, have we been led down the primrose path?"

"Yeah, I know what you mean. This still doesn't sit well," Nick admitted.

"Here's another thing that I'm wondering. Why did they suspect the kid in the first place?" Johnson scratched his head.

"I remember that part. The file said that a bit earlier, the housekeeper was vacuuming downstairs. Lawrence had taken the car and gone out to the store. Xander was in his studio and Oscar was down the hall in the study. Could have happened then. They said that Xander could have pushed him out while the housekeeper was vacuuming. Xander and the housekeeper went for walk, leaving from the door on the opposite side of the house. The body could have been on the ground already. We don't know exact time of death, and their walk only lasted about half an hour." Nick explained.

"Right. But if that's the case, how could the housekeeper have heard glass breaking and the scream right after?"

"Maybe she thought she heard glass breaking but didn't. The power of suggestion. She sees a broken window that obviously someone has come through, and imagines she heard it break. And maybe the scream was Lawrence, crying out for help. That's how they reasoned it out originally to point the finger at Xander." Nick said.

"True," replied Johnson. "But if you're right about the fact that there's very little blood in the sketch, there's no way he did it. Couldn't have."

Nick found himself nodding his head in agreement. Again.

Dulcie sat in her office with the formidable Edith Bernstein. They had just watched the mini-documentary on Xander. Edith nodded her head in approval. "Yes. Use it. That psychologist narrating is an ass, but he says the right things."

Dulcie coughed to hide a laugh.

Edith sat back in her chair. Dulcie realized that it was the first time she had ever seen Edith Bernstein sit back. The woman was normally sitting so erectly that she looked like she would fall over.

"It's a bad business all around," she clucked. "I'm sure Lawrence didn't do it, but somebody did. My brother wouldn't just hurl himself out the window. He was too in love with himself to do that."

"I didn't know him, but it does all seem odd. Unfinished," Dulcie added.

"Yes, that's a good word," Edith stated. "Question is, what kind of finish will it have?"

Dulcie sat back in her chair also, unconsciously mimicking Edith's stance. She folded her arms. "Do you feel at all nervous or threatened there, especially with Lawrence back in the house?" she asked.

"No. Not a hair," Edith chortled. "And that's the odd thing about it."

After several moments, Dulcie said, "Mrs. Bernstein, what do you know about Giselle?"

Edith thought back. She had only met Giselle once or twice before moving in to the house with her, but had known about her for years, of course. "Good woman. Dotes over Xander. Has served the family well. Few would have put up with it."

"Yes, and that's why I ask the question. Do you know her background?" Dulcie asked.

Edith squinted her eyes. "Let me see, from Quebec, but you knew that of course. Last name Guerrette. I think I heard someone say once she was raised by her grandmother? When Lily died, that's Oscar's wife, Giselle kept the household running. Gisa was failing pretty rapidly at that point."

"And Gisa was Xander's mother, Lawrence's wife, right?" Dulcie asked.

"Yes. Not much use in the end, God rest her soul, but I think she tried in the beginning."

Dulcie had never had such a long conversation with Edith Bernstein. She glanced around her office and saw the painting that Edith had brought to her attention initially. "Mrs. Bernstein, who's shadow do you think that is in the painting?"

"Haven't a clue."

"Has Giselle seen it?" The question was simple, but its impact gradually increased on Edith. Dulcie watched the light in her spark, then begin to burn brighter as she considered its implications.

"No. She has not. She has not seen it. And you think…" Edith trailed off, not willing to say the rest. "I can't see it, though. She's been so loyal to the family."

"Maybe that's exactly why?" Dulcie countered. "Maybe she is so loyal to the family that when she saw the threat of Oscar Bernstein increase, she took matters into her own hands?"

"If that's true, why would she have allowed Lawrence to go to prison?"

"From what I understand," Dulcie replied. "Giselle's loyalty isn't necessarily to the family. Her loyalty is to Xander."

Edith stood rapidly, scraping the chair behind her. Dulcie jumped at the sound. "I have to go," Edith announced and strode from the room.

Well! Dulcie thought. *That was odd!* Then again, Edith was an odd woman. Dulcie looked up as she heard footsteps at her doorway, half expecting to see Edith come in again. Instead her brother Dan came into the room.

"Who was that?" he said, jerking his thumb over his shoulder to point. "She nearly ran me over!"

"*That*," Dulcie paused for emphasis, "Was the formidable Edith Bernstein. Consider yourself lucky." She joked. "Don't you remember her from the other day when Xander painted you?"

"Nope," Dan answered as he sauntered in and slumped into the chair that Edith had recently vacated. "What's her story?" he asked.

"You don't have enough time, Dan." She saw him look at his watch. "Trust me! But we just had the oddest conversation, which is saying something because every conversation with her is odd."

Dan sat up. "Tell me."

Dulcie sighed, thinking for a moment. Where to begin? "She's Xander Bellamy's great aunt. She only recently came into that household when the father was carted off to prison."

"For a crime he didn't commit, but confessed to," Dan said.

"Right. The other person in the saga is Giselle, the housekeeper," Dulcie continued.

"Ah, yes. The lovely Giselle! I remember her from the filming," Dan said.

"Of course you do," Dulcie said, shaking her head with resignation. Dan was well known for appreciating a pretty face. "Just now with Edith Bernstein, I was trying to get all of the family connections straight, especially since half of them are dead now."

"Okay, lay it on me," Dan offered.

Dulcie took a deep breath. "First, there's Oscar. He was married to a woman named Lily. She already had a daughter, Gisa…"

"What? Wait a second. She already had a daughter?"

"Yes," Dulcie answered.

"So is that Xander's mother?"

"Yes," Dulcie replied again. "Oscar is, was, her step-father.

"There's the first strange thing. But keep going," Dan interjected.

"Gisa eventually met Lawrence and they were married. Then Xander was born," Dulcie said.

"So when did Giselle come into the picture?" asked Dan

"I'm not sure but it was at least when Xander was a tiny baby. She's been with him pretty much from the beginning. So, Xander's condition becomes apparent pretty early on. The family is living with Oscar who pays all the bills. He also makes their lives miserable. Gisa begins spiraling into a rapid decline and eventually dies from a combination of alcohol and sleeping pills."

"And Giselle was already around by then?" Dan asked.

"Yes," Dulcie said.

"What kind of a name is Gisa?" Dan mused. "Sounds Middle Eastern or something."

"You're thinking of Gaza," Dulcie replied. "I think it's German or maybe Austrian?"

"You're the intellectual of the family," Dan teased.

"All right, fine. Now I have to look it up." Dulcie sat forward and opened her laptop. "Yes, I'm right, of course. Here it is. Gisa, a German name for a girl that translates to…" Dulcie looked up at Dan. "Now that's interesting!" she exclaimed.

"What? What is it?" he demanded.

"It translates to *Giselle*."

That evening the doorbell rang at Dulcie's townhouse. The building was an old, brick structure set among an entire street of townhouses in one of the city's older districts. Not only had Dulcie fallen in love with it the first time she saw it, but it was within walking distance of the museum which made it all the more perfect. She hurried to the door and swung it open without even peeking through the window to see who it was.

Nick stood on the steps with a large paper bag. Dulcie quickly grabbed it, spun around, and put it on the kitchen counter. She put both hands on the top and ripped the bag open. Nick had seen her do this before, but it always startled him a bit. She had once told him it was the easiest way to get at the containers. They were always packed tightly into the bag. Nick suspected that she just liked ripping the bag open.

"I want you to know that you put my high school French to the test," Dulcie remarked. "I learned Italian in college, and I kept throwing in things like *grazie* instead of *merci*."

"I'm very sorry to have caused difficulty," Nick teased.

Dulcie ignored him. She handed him a tray and said, "Take everything to the table please. I'll get wine." Nick did so obediently.

Dulcie stepped out of the kitchen a moment later with a bottle of Montepulciano d'Abruzzo. "I just got some of that, too!" Nick commented.

"It's my current favorite," Dulcie replied. "I've been in an Italian mode lately. Thus my difficulty with the French this afternoon," she added.

"I am very appreciative, however," Nick said. He opened several boxes, handed one to Dulcie, and took one for himself. Dulcie looked inside hers and sighed. Chicken fried rice.

"You're going to be very appreciative," she said after several bites. "I tracked down Lily Bernstein through the records office in Quebec. It seems that prior to marrying Oscar, she was Lily Harmon. And prior to that, she was Lily Guerrette." Nick started to speak, but Dulcie held up her hand to stop him. "Wait! There's more! Lily Harmon had twins. One was named Gisa Harmon. The other was adopted by her grandmother…"

"And let me guess. Her name was Giselle Guerrette!" Nick exclaimed.

Dulcie simply nodded, smiled, and dug deeper into her fried rice.

"Well! That puts a spin on things! So Giselle is really Xander's aunt, and Lawrence's sister-in-law! Wow!" Nick put down his chopsticks and tapped his fingers on the table. "Wow!" he repeated. "So the question now is, who knew? Did anyone know? She must have known, certainly. It couldn't be that big of a coincidence that she just happens to end up in the same household as her sister."

"You wouldn't think so," Dulcie said. She put down the now empty container of fried rice and opened a bag of egg rolls.

Nick was now ignoring the food. "I can only imagine that as Lily's daughter, Gisa's sister, *and* Xander's aunt, she must have been harboring a lot of hatred for Oscar."

Dulcie nodded, her mouth full. "Ummmhmmm," was all she managed to get out in response.

Nick was oblivious. "It would explain the bond she had with Xander, too. She took more interest in him than seemed normal." He walked across to the window. It was dark. Sunsets were very early now that they were well into autumn. "This just got complicated," he murmured.

Dulcie poured more wine. "It did? I thought it just got easier!" she countered.

Nick came back to the table. "You're right, but so am I. We now have a very strong motive for one person in particular to have killed Oscar. The question is, does she have a motive to kill anyone else? What about Lawrence? Is he the next victim? After all, he was there when both Giselle's mother and sister died. He did nothing."

"What could he do?" asked Dulcie.

"Probably not much, but Giselle may not see it that way. Dulcie, do you know if Giselle has seen that painting? The one of Lawrence leaving the room and Oscar laughing?"

Dulcie thought for a moment. "I don't think so. Edith Bernstein brought it to me. She found it in a stack of paintings in Xander's studio. She took it to her room afterward which is where I saw it. Then she gave it to me so that I could bring it to my office."

"Why did she do that?" Nick wondered.

"I'm not sure. Maybe she thought I could see something in it that she couldn't? Or maybe even that I would show it to the police?"

Nick sipped his wine for a moment. "I think I know what we have to do. Can I meet you at your office in the morning? Do you have any free time?" Nick asked.

"Let me check my schedule," Dulcie went to her desk and flipped open her laptop. "I have an hour free at ten o'clock. Would that work?"

"Hopefully. I'll let you know in the morning." He started to pick up his dinner things, but Dulcie waved him off. "No, no! You brought all of this over! I'll take care of clean-up. Thank you, by the way. For dinner."

"Thank you, for the insight. And the wine. And the good company." He put on his jacket but hesitated as he walked to the door. "Dulcie, I mean that. You're really good company," he confessed.

She smiled. "You are too, Nick." He opened the door as she turned on the outside light. "I'll see you tomorrow."

"You bet. 'Night." His arm jerked in a half-wave. He knew it looked awkward, but it was an attempt to hide its initial motion. He had so wanted to feel how soft her hair was.

CHAPTER TEN

At ten o'clock the next morning, Rachel bounced in to Dulcie's office. "Visitors!" she announced.

"Thank you, Rachel. And who might they be?"

Rachel stepped back. "These guys," she said, walking by Nick and Lawrence Bellamy who had just entered the office.

"Thank you Rachel. As always you are a wealth of knowledge and decorum!" Dulcie called out after her.

"I do what I can!" she called back from the hallway.

"She really is a very good assistant," Dulcie laughed. "In spite of the sass."

Nick chuckled. "I hope you don't mind that I've brought a guest."

"Not at all," Dulcie replied. She came around her desk and shook hands with Lawrence. He towered over her. Her fingers looked like a child's compared to his, but his handshake was gentle. "What can I do for you two?"

"I'm wondering if we can see the painting that Xander made," Nick asked. "The one in Oscar Bernstein's study."

"Yes, absolutely," Dulcie replied turning to a table in the corner. Several canvases were propped against the wall on it. She rearranged them, bringing the requested work to the front.

Lawrence stepped forward. "I do remember," he said quietly. "That was the last argument I had with Oscar. It was the day he died. I didn't realize that Xander saw us in there." Lawrence thought of the sketchbook Xander had made, the fear he must have understood. "I wish I could have done more for my son. I wish I had just taken him away…," his voice quavered.

Dulcie began to speak, to reassure him, but Nick shook his head. "Lawrence, I want you to look at this carefully. Do you see this shadow over here."

Lawrence leaned over and studied the painting. "Yes," he replied simply.

"It looks like the shadow of a person," Nick said.

"It is," Lawrence replied.

"Can you tell us who was in the room with Oscar when you left?" Nick asked.

Lawrence's voice was soft. Barely audible. "Giselle," he whispered.

"Means, motive, and opportunity," Nick said after Lawrence had left. Giselle had the means. It wouldn't have taken much, especially in a fit of rage, for her to push Oscar out the window. He wasn't a big man, and he was old."

"True. She had the motive, certainly. Oscar was a major factor in her sister's death, and he sounds like he was pretty horrible when it came to Xander," Dulcie added.

"So we're down to opportunity. She had that as well."

"She did?" Dulcie exclaimed. "But I thought that she and Xander..."

"That's her story. She could have pushed him out the window earlier. She knew Lawrence had gone out and she knew approximately when he would be back. She could have pushed Oscar, taken Xander for a quick walk, and come back to find Oscar dead."

Dulcie pondered this new scenario. "Yes, she could have done that. Do you have that sketchbook with you, by any chance?"

"Actually I do. I brought in case we wanted to look at it along with the painting." He fished through a canvas bag on the floor beside him. Dulcie realized that Nick never carried anything. Was that part of the police thing? Were both hands supposed to be free at all times?

Nick interrupted her thoughts and handed her the book. Dulcie opened it from the back to look at the image of Lawrence and Oscar's body. She very carefully examined one object and the next, scrutinizing the detail. It all seemed to fit, until... there!

Yes, that was it. She turned the page to look at the back of the paper. Yes, that confirmed it.

"What are you doing?" Nick asked.

"I'm doing what I should have done before. I'm looking at the technique and not the subject. And what I see is exactly what I know that that I should have expected to see."

"I'm confused," Nick confessed.

"Look at the way Xander draws. He's outlined everything, almost like a cartoon. It doesn't look cartoonish because he show's detail so well, but the outline is there on everything in the picture. But look at the shadow in the window. No outline."

Nick leaned over the drawing. His nose was almost on the paper. "You're right!"

"And look at this." Dulcie turned the page over. "You can see consistent indentations on the back of the paper. He doesn't press very hard. But again, look at the shadow. You can feel it bump out on the back." She ran her fingers across it. Involuntarily, Nick did the same.

"So this means that the shadow might have been added later," Nick reasoned.

"Yes, and it means that most likely, Xander didn't draw the shadow," Dulcie said. "To my knowledge, only two people have seen this book other than you and I. Lawrence, and…"

"Giselle," Nick finished the sentence.

Dulcie felt sick. The one person that had cared for Xander. The one person who truly understood him. They couldn't just rip her away like that. What would happen to him? It would be even worse than his father being taken away. Yet she had betrayed Dulcie's trust. She had betrayed everyone's trust. Dulcie still couldn't believe it, but Giselle must have done it. She must have pushed Oscar out the window in a fit of rage or even despair.

Did she feel justified killing him? When Lawrence went to prison for her crime, what did she feel then? How could she have let that happen? But Dulcie understood. Giselle was Xander's aunt, just as Edith was Xander's aunt. The aunties close ranks, more so than any other blood relation, when the children have to be protected. It happened not only with humans, but other species as well. Dulcie had read that it was undoubtedly biological in some way. She wondered if Edith knew or suspected anything about Giselle.

Nick was still talking. "I need to find Johnson. We have to go through the file, get everyone's story again." His mind was already spinning.

"Unless I get Giselle to confess," Dulcie said.

"What? How is that even possible? She didn't say anything before. Why would she now?"

"Because I know. Because I have all of the pieces that, together, form the proof. Because I can convince her that if she does confess, it will be easier for her. The sentence could be more lenient."

"How... how do you propose to do this?" Nick stammered.

"I'll go to their house. I'll bring the painting and the sketch. I'll record the conversation."

"Oh no! No undercover work for you, Dulcie!"

"All right. Fine. You can be in the next room or the hallway or wherever." Dulcie was thoughtful for a moment. "You know, we should get Edith's help, too. She's brusque, but I know she'd see this whole situation the right way."

Nick was silent. Then he reached into his pocket for his phone. "I have to call Johnson," he said. "You call dear Aunt Edith."

An hour later, Dulcie approached the house of Xander Bellamy carrying his painting and sketchbook. She rang the bell. Giselle came to the door.

"*Dul-cee, quelle surprise!*" she said by way of greeting.

"Yes, I spoke to Edith," Dulcie wasn't sure if Giselle knew that Dulcie and Edith had spoken earlier. "She didn't tell you I'd be here, evidently."

"*Non*, but come in. I see you have Xander's artworks. Are you returning them?"

"Yes," Dulcie lied. "Could I bring them upstairs?" Dulcie had covered the large canvas with cloth so that Giselle could not see what it was. She hoped that Giselle would think it was the painting that Xander had made of Dulcie.

"Of course," Giselle said. "Follow me." They went to Xander's studio.

Downstairs, Dulcie heard the door open softly, then close. She put down Xander's things and said, "Giselle, I know this sounds odd, but could I see Oscar's studio one more time? I saw something in the painting Xander did that I wanted to look at."

Giselle looked puzzled, but waved Dulcie through toward the room, then followed her in.

Dulcie stopped and looked around for several moments. "Giselle, I know it was horrible living with Oscar," she began.

"*Oui*. He was a terrible man. One had to cope."

Dulcie hoped that Nick was in the hallway, listening. She thought she had given him enough time to come upstairs. "It must have been terrible, knowing Oscar had contributed to those deaths."

"You mean Xander's *mère*?"

"Yes, I mean Xander's mother Your sister. I also mean Xander's grandmother, Lily, who was your mother."

Giselle turned white. She swayed. Dulcie thought she was going to fall over. Giselle collapsed into a chair. "You know my secret," she whispered.

"Yes," Dulcie said quietly. "That's why you cared about Xander, truly loved him, so much. That's why you must have snapped when you were in this room with Oscar on the last day of his life."

Giselle's eyes were wide. "How did you know…?"

"Because Gisa and Giselle are the same name in different languages. The records office in Quebec confirmed the rest. More importantly, however, is that Xander made a painting. He had walked by the room the day that Oscar was killed. He saw his father, and his grandfather, but not the third person in the room. He simply saw a shadow of the third person. Today, Lawrence saw that painting. He said that the shadow was you."

Giselle had begun to cry. Tears streamed down her face. "*Oui!* I was in the room! He was terrible that day! I was so angry and hurt! But you think…" she sobbed,

"You think I killed him? *Non!* I did not! I could not! I hated him with all of the venom in my heart, but I could not have done such a thing as push him out the window! I couldn't!"

Dulcie had not anticipated this reaction. Worse, she was now beginning to believe Giselle. She turned and looked out the window, her mind reeling. Bright sunshine streamed through the trees and danced on the paved driveway below. A squirrel hopped from a branch just outside the window down to a bush, then to the ground where it ran along through what was left of the summer grass.

It was then that Dulcie knew. Without question, she knew. She turned back to Giselle slowly. "I believe you," she said. "You could not have done it. But I know who did."

A large form emerged from the shadows at the back of the room. Dulcie gasped as Lawrence Bellamy moved toward her. Nick sensed someone else moving in the room and stepped into the doorway. Dulcie did not look at him, but Nick knew she wanted him to stop. He froze. Neither Lawrence nor Giselle knew Nick was there.

"You were telling the truth after all, Lawrence, weren't you," Dulcie said. The huge man stepped closer toward her. Dulcie's heart thudded, but she held her ground. "You confessed, but no one believed you."

He took another step toward her.

"You did push Oscar through the window. You were standing over him when Giselle and Xander came up the path. It was just as they said, just as Xander had drawn. And you were able to do this because *you jumped out of the window as soon as Oscar fell.* You're so tall that it wasn't nearly as much of a fall, and you were able to land on your feet so you had less chance of getting hurt."

Lawrence closed the gap between them, and Nick raced into the room followed by Johnson and Edith. Nick was about to grab Lawrence when he stepped around Dulcie without touching her and walked up to the window. Everyone froze. Lawrence raised his long arm and pointed.

"There," he said. "I landed right there."

Johnson drove Dulcie's car back into the city. Dulcie was shaken by the whole encounter. It had not gone according to plan. She sat in the back seat with Nick. "That was strange," she said. "Tell me why you didn't arrest Lawrence Bellamy?"

Johnson looked at Nick in the rear view mirror. "We managed to exonerate him after the first confession, assuming that it was false. We had what we thought was convincing evidence, Xander's sketch, showing that he could not have done it, and he had a compelling reason for making a false confession in that he thought they were going to accuse Xander," Nick said.

"Looks like we were wrong," Johnson added.

"You weren't exactly wrong," Dulcie contradicted him. "Didn't Giselle tamper with the evidence by drawing in that shadow?"

"Yes, but by then the case had been closed. That sketchbook was never used as evidence in the trial. True, we've opened another case to look into the matter, but a good lawyer would be able to shut us down. Evidence has been handled by too many people. Plus, you can't convict someone of the same crime twice."

"Chief is gonna kill us," Johnson mumbled.

"Maybe not," Nick said. "We kept everything pretty low key. This could stay under wraps, too. We'll be in the doghouse for a while, but we've solved some pretty tough cases for him and made him look good. We're allowed a mistake once in a while. No one in that household is going to talk about it – I'm pretty certain of that. Besides, I don't think Lawrence Bellamy is exactly a threat to anyone."

"Even though he's huge! Have you ever seen anyone that big? I mean, seriously!" Johnson marveled. "Man, if I was that big, I could eat all day long," he added wistfully.

Dulcie laughed. She was beginning to relax at last. "Adam, is that what all the walking has been about?"

"Well, sorta. I mean… dammit," he swore softly. "Nick, you tell her."

Nick groaned. "Fine. You see, it seems that our friend here made a bet with his wife. She challenged him to lose ten pounds in one month, or walk 300,000 steps."

"That seems like a pretty good challenge. But I assume the stakes are high?"

Johnson just grunted from the front seat.

"You could say that," Nick snickered. "If he wins, they go to Florida for a week to see the Red Sox at spring training."

"Including VIP tickets!" Johnson chimed in.

"Including VIP tickets," Nick repeated.

"And if he loses?" Dulcie asked.

"That's the kicker. Then it will be... what was it Johnson?" Nick grinned at Dulcie.

They heard something from the front seat.

"What was that?" Nick said. "We couldn't hear you!"

"La Dolce Vita Spa and Weight Loss Center!" Johnson bellowed. "And I'll drive this car right off the road unless you promise right now never to tell a living soul!!"

Dulcie laughed the rest of the way home.

⚃

The Outsider Art exhibit continued according to plan. Dulcie felt exhausted, but she was pleased with the outcome. She had invited Xander and his family to attend of course, but they still weren't sure whether they should. Or could.

On the day of the opening, Dulcie hurried around the main hall of the museum all afternoon checking on details. Pictures were hung, lights installed and aimed, sculptural pieces stood on platforms... yes, it was all in place. Dulcie walked slowly through the exhibit space, double and triple checking every detail, then ticking each off on a clipboard. She dropped her pen and as she reached down to pick it up noticed her shoes. She let out an exasperated moan.

"What's up?" Rachel's voice carried through the empty room.

Dulcie looked at her ruefully. "I do this every time, don't I," she nearly wailed.

Rachel giggled. "You mean, you forgot your outfit? Again?"

Dulcie nodded. "I don't have time to get home and change, either." She looked down at her shoes again. Scuffed, tan leather ballet flats. They would never do.

"Don't worry. I can run to your place and get some clothes. Any thoughts, or shall I just put together something fabulous?"

"I doubt you can find that in my closet," Dulcie said. "However, yes, I would love it if you could do that. My keys are in my purse. Bottom left drawer of the desk."

"I know!" Rachel replied. "Won't be a minute!"

Dulcie was more than a little nervous thinking of the sort of outfit Rachel would choose. Whatever it was, Dulcie would be stuck with it.

Half an hour before the opening was scheduled to begin, Dulcie saw a large shadow lurking in the foyer outside the front door. She knew of only one person that could possibly make a shadow of that size: Lawrence Bellamy. Dulcie glanced down at the dress Rachel had chosen for her. Made of a deep teal colored silk, it was fitted on the top and flared out to a full skirt on the bottom with snug short sleeves and a deeply scooped neck in the front and back. Rachel had paired it with plain black pumps. When Dulcie had seen the dress on the rack it reminded her of something from the 1960s. It was the one item in her closet that she was still trying to work up the courage to wear. She had no idea why she had bought it. Perhaps Rachel somehow knew this? Dulcie smoothed out her skirt and went to the door.

Lawrence stood with the others from his household: Giselle, Edith, and Xander. They looked much more relaxed, more like a family, than the last time Dulcie had seen them.

"Would you like to sneak in early?" she said as she opened the door.

"We were hoping we could," Lawrence said. He held the door for the others as they entered. Dulcie made sure that it closed and locked behind them.

"Do you want the guided tour, or would you just like to look on your own?" she asked.

"On our own," Edith barked. "You've got more than enough to do right now," she added. The caterers were putting out snacks on several tables, and Dulcie kept glancing over to see if everything was in the right place.

"Yes, that would be best. I'll find you in a few minutes," she said.

Giselle had not spoken. After their last encounter, Dulcie would have been surprised if Giselle ever spoke to her again. After all, Dulcie had accused her of murdering Oscar Bernstein, and had police hiding, waiting to pounce on her and make an arrest. It wasn't exactly endearing behavior on Dulcie's part.

Dulcie took care of the final details for the opening checked her dress and make-up one last time in her office mirror, and went in to the exhibit. Xander and his father were standing in front of Xander's work. The video was on a continuous loop and they could hear Dr. Raymond Armand's voice droning on. Xander stared at it blankly. Edith stood in front of the bottle-cap and chewing-gum Statue of Liberty looking appalled. Giselle was at the opposite end of the gallery.

Dulcie quietly approached her. "Giselle," she said as she came near, "I'm so sorry."

Giselle did not look up. Dulcie thought that she would turn away, refusing to speak with her. After what seemed a very long time she said, "No, it is I who should be sorry."

Giselle didn't see the look of surprise on Dulcie's face, but she knew it was there. "I knew what had happened. I did not know exactly how, or the details, or the fact that Lawrence was even guilty, but deep down I knew. That is why I altered the drawing. That was wrong. But it was the only way I could see that would bring him back to Xander."

Now she did look up at Dulcie. Her eyes welled with tears, but she fought to keep them in check. "You see, I love him so much. Xander. And in a way, I have grown to love Lawrence, too. They are gentle souls. The way that they were treated would not be right for any person, but it was especially wrong for people like them. I had to watch over them." Giselle looked over at a nearby bench and said, "Do you mind if we sit?"

Dulcie glanced at her dress, wondering if it would wrinkle, then decided that she didn't care. "Of course," she said.

Giselle slid onto the bench as Dulcie perched on the edge. Giselle continued," My sister and I were very different. Technically we were twins, but fraternal of course. We do not look alike. My mother kept Gisa because she was the smaller, more needy child from the very beginning. The belief was that with her own mother, Gisa would become more strong. I was always more independent, so I was sent to live with my grandmother. She was a kind, loving woman. I had a good childhood." Giselle stopped.

Dulcie nodded. She was close to her own brother. She understood.

"Gisa and I decided that we should not tell anyone that I was her sister. I came to America to live with her not because she wanted a housekeeper but because she wanted me there. She was frightened. Oscar Bernstein was a terrible man. I know that in some way, he caused our mother's death, and he drove Gisa to hers as well. The more I saw Xander, my only remaining family, the more I felt that I had to protect him."

Dulcie was overwhelmed by Giselle's story, and swallowed hard in a futile attempt to eliminate the lump from her throat. "You did well," she finally managed to say. "You did protect him. You and Lawrence have been his whole world. I know that he must, on some level, understand and appreciate that."

Giselle sniffed, forcing herself to remain in control. "I do not need any of that, any appreciation from others," she said. "I just need to know that he is safe and content."

Content. It wasn't the same as happy. Xander might not ever understand happiness but Dulcie was sure that he knew what it was like to feel content. She reached over and took Giselle's hand, squeezing it briefly in her own. "Please come and see me again here. I think Xander would like it. And I would love to be able to talk with you more, too."

Giselle blinked away tears and nodded. "I would like that as well," she said softly.

Dulcie stood, leaving her to collect her thoughts. She joined Lawrence and Xander. Looking pointedly at Xander she said, "I hope you like this. You did a wonderful job. I think so many people will understand artists like you because of it." Xander continued to stare blankly at the video screen.

Dulcie looked up at Lawrence. "Stay as long as you like," she said. "I need to get back to things."

"Of course," he said quietly.

"Come back again," she added. Lawrence smiled and put a protective hand on Xander's shoulder.

Dulcie walked back to the main hall where the caterers were noisily completing their setup. One glanced at Dulcie and said, "Would you like some champagne?"

"You read my mind!" she answered.

He handed her a tall, cool glass. Sipping it, and trying not to sneeze from the bubbles, she glanced through the still-locked front doors. She saw Nick standing outside, waiting for the opening to begin. Dulcie caught his eye, then motioned to the guard nearby to let Nick in.

He squeezed quickly through the door and strode across the room. "Dulcie, you look amazing," he said with sincerity.

"Well, I forgot my clothes to change into and sent Rachel to my house to get something, so she picked this out. I don't think I would have chosen it, but…" she tried to stop herself from babbling. Looking down, she took a deep breath. Her eyes met his again. "Thank you!" she answered simply. "I should have said that in the first place!"

A waiter came by with a tray of champagne glasses. Nick happily took one. "Everything seems to be going well. Did you have any more difficulties with this exhibit?"

Dulcie nearly snorted her champagne. *Difficulties* would be an understatement for what they had gone through. "No, once we solved a murder, everything was smooth sailing!" she joked.

Speaking of which…" Nick began looking around them.

"Yes, they're here," Dulcie said. "I let them come in early. I thought it would be easier. They're in the gallery." She pointed behind him.

"I'll leave them be. They've been through enough. Just let them enjoy," he said. As he finished speaking, Lawrence and the others emerged from the new exhibit. They joined Dulcie and Nick.

"Well, it was certainly unorthodox, but you did help Lawrence, and all of us, in the end. So, my thanks for that," Edith barked at Nick.

He wasn't sure what to say. He certainly couldn't condone murder, or openly support a murderer, but life wasn't always quite that clear-cut.

Dulcie came to his rescue. "Did you enjoy the exhibit?" she said, very obviously changing the subject.

"Everything but that big Statue of Liberty thing!" Edith boomed. "That's just an abomination!"

"Yes," Dulcie said tactfully, "It's difficult to define art sometimes. But I think the person who created it was, in his own way, an artist. Just as Xander is."

The doors had opened and all of the invited guests for the opening began to make their way in. They were happy, talking loudly, lingering over the hors d'oeuvres and eventually meandering into the gallery to see the exhibit.

Lawrence Bellamy corralled his family and turned toward the door. "We must go," he said to Dulcie. "Thank you for letting us come in early, and thank you for showing Xander's gift so positively."

Dulcie nodded. "It's my pleasure," she said simply. As they crossed the large room, Xander suddenly stopped. He turned back around. Dulcie watched him, curious as to what he would do. He walked back to her and for a brief moment Dulcie thought he might have even made eye contact. She wasn't sure. His face now simply held his usual distant gaze. Yet, while he stood there, he lifted his hand, and turned it so that it opened, palm up. Then he slowly swiveled back around toward the door and walked away.

Giselle had called it *espérance*. Hope. For Xander, Dulcie knew that they had every reason to believe that this was true.

During the next hour Dulcie saw Dr. Raymond Armand come in. He was talking with two of the more wealthy museum patrons who looked attentive yet bored. She tried to hide a smirk but Nick caught her. He touched her elbow and guided her away from the others she had been talking with. "Am I correct in assuming that the good Dr. Armand has an interest in you?" It was a very direct question, and he held his breath.

"I'm not sure if the present tense is correct," she replied, sipping her champagne. "I don't think I've given any encouragement."

"Is encouragement required in this case?" Nick asked innocently.

"Good point," Dulcie murmured.

Raymond had spotted her and came over to join them. He nodded at Nick dismissively, then quickly took Dulcie's hand and kissed it. "You look exquisite Dr. Chambers!" he said, without letting go of her hand. He had intended the use of her title as a way to put down Nick. Even though Raymond didn't consider Dulcie's doctorate to be as lofty as his, he was practically in medicine after all, they both had the degree, which was far better than this lowly policeman could hope for, he was sure.

Dulcie used it to her advantage. "You may remember meeting Dr. Nicholas Black?" She effectively removed her hand from Raymond's by gesturing toward Nick.

"*Doctor* Black?" Raymond responded with eyebrows raised, unable to hide his disbelief.

"Yes," Dulcie jumped in before Nick could say anything. "Like you and I, Nick has a doctorate as well. You earned it at Harvard, if I recall correctly Nick?" she asked innocently as she turned toward him.

Nick nodded, realizing where she was going with the conversation. "Dulcie, I don't think I know where you want to graduate school," he replied inquiringly. He actually knew full well where she had gone.

"Oxford. Yes, yes, I jumped the pond!" she said, pretending to cut off anything he was about to say. "And don't give me any grief about American vs. British schools!" she teased. She turned to Raymond.

He knew what the next question would be and had no intention of divulging where he had earned his doctorate. He fought hard to control his ego and quickly said, "It was certainly interesting working on this project. I'm happy that it turned out so well. I'll forward my bill for the consulting services next week." He glanced at Nick. "Good to meet you," Raymond added even though they had already met before.

Dulcie nodded and smiled. Nick raised his glass tactfully and murmured, "Pleasure." Dr. Raymond Armand sauntered away, disgusted with both of them.

"Oh my," said Dulcie. "I'm sure that was wrong, but he really needed to be stopped."

Nick had turned his back to the room so that no one would see his expression. He didn't like to laugh at someone else's discomfort, but in this case he couldn't help it. "Yes, that was pretty bad, Dulcie. But he did deserve it. At least this once. I have to say also, that's the first time I've ever been called doctor! And hopefully the last."

"Well, you've earned it, obviously…" she began

"I know, but it doesn't fit anymore with who I am or what I want now," he interjected.

Dulcie sipped her champagne thoughtfully. She had already been bold this evening. Why not keep going? "What do you want now, Nick?" she asked. She gazed across the room casually. Waiting.

Nick stared into his champagne glass, watching the bubbles float to the surface. What had she just said? Okay, that was stupid. He knew what she had said. What did she mean? He glanced up at her. A soft smile had spread across her lips. His breath caught in his throat.

"What I want…" he began, then stopped. He took another sip of champagne. It gave him more courage. "What I want is to have dinner later this evening with a beautiful and brilliant woman who has dark hair and is wearing a green dress." He held his breath.

Dulcie was unprepared for the massive flush of color that washed over her. She wanted to put the chilly champagne glass against her cheeks to cool them down. She hoped that it wasn't too obvious. "Oh dear," she said looking down at herself. "This isn't green, it's teal. I guess I'm immediately out of contention then."

"Did I say a green dress? I meant a teal dress," he managed to reply.

Dulcie slowly leaned forward and whispered in his ear, "I'd love to!" Then she stepped away and moved among the groups of chattering people.

Nick found himself exhaling very, very slowly as he forced himself to stay where he was and not follow her like a puppy. But he wasn't as successful at removing the goofy smile that was stuck on his face for the rest of the evening.

A DULCIE CHAMBERS MUSEUM MYSTERY
KERRY J CHARLES
LAST OF THE VINTAGE

LAST OF THE VINTAGE

CHAPTER 1

The waves crashed against the nearby rocks, dangerously close to the tiny cottage. The entire house shook again and again with an ominous predictability. In the seven years of Hazel's entire existence living on the island, she had never heard waves like these before.

She had wanted to go outside to see them, but her mother wouldn't let her. "No," her mother had said firmly. "Besides, there's no moon. You can't see anything, anyway."

This was true. Thick black clouds had rolled in during the afternoon and the winds howled along with them, all through the night. The first hint of light now crept above the horizon, and Hazel couldn't hold back any longer. She slowly eased herself out of the bed, hoping that her mother wouldn't wake up just yet.

Her mother had been awake for nearly the entire night. She had shielded the light of the paraffin lamp so that it wouldn't shine directly toward the bed. She sat at the table with her book, pretending to read. Hazel knew that she wasn't. Her mother hadn't turned a single page.

Hazel normally slept in the loft upstairs, except during storms. Then she slept in the bigger bed downstairs, at her mother's insistence. All that her mother could picture was the roof coming off the house or a tall pine tree falling through it.

Hazel crept toward the door and opened it. She slipped outside. The air was warm and wet, strange for October. She could feel the crash of the surf through the stone step beneath her bare feet. From her vantage point, she could easily see the waves. They were massive, at least four or five times taller than she was. A shiver ran down her spine.

She followed the swells backward, out toward the open ocean. Something strange caught her eye farther away. It looked like the mast of a ship, except sideways. She squinted in the early dawn light. The object disappeared, then reappeared with each swell. She thought she could see a white sail fluttering around it.

The waves followed the usual routine of several comparatively smaller swells followed by one or two much larger ones. As she watched, a bigger wave hit the object and it disappeared. It bobbed back up again only to be hit by another large wave. She lost sight of the object again and stood watching, waiting for it to reappear. It never did.

Hazel stood on the front step for several more minutes wondering what she had just seen. Finally she convinced herself that it was simply a floating log with seagulls flying around it. She had seen debris like that in the water before, and gulls circled anything bobbing around, always looking for an easy meal. She nodded once, happy with her conclusion, yawned, then tiptoed back inside. She slid into bed again beside her mother and fell back asleep.

Dulcie rummaged through the closet and found her down vest. She slipped into it, zipped it all the way up, then put her winter coat on over it. She was already wearing heavy boots. The coat came down below her knees, almost reaching the tops of the boots. Next she pulled on a knit hat, flipped her hood up over it, then wrapped a scarf around her neck several times until it covered the entire lower half of her face. She looked in the mirror and laughed. Only her eyes and her hands were visible. She made sure that her bag was securely closed, then put on heavy gloves. Slinging the bag over one arm she turned to open the door. She couldn't grip the knob so she had to take off one glove, grab the knob again, open the door, then put the glove back on. "And we have two more months of this?" she said out loud.

She stepped outside, closing the door firmly behind her, making sure that it was locked. The first breath that she inhaled made her gasp. Her scarf had slipped down, and the frigid air hit her lungs like a hammer. They now felt like Styrofoam. Her nose seemed to be frozen from the inside as well. She shoved the scarf up with her gloved hand and began to trudge down the street.

Dulcie hadn't even attempted to start her vehicle that morning. The old Jeep Wrangler that she loved had seen better days. She knew it would be an exercise in futility to listen to the starter grind over and over again with absolutely no hope of it kicking the engine into action. All it would do was wear down the battery.

She scuffled down the street, walking quickly to stay warm. Two below, the thermometer had read. It didn't matter. Once you reach a certain state of coldness it all feels the same. Normally the walk took ten minutes. Today it was much quicker since she nearly jogged the entire distance.

Oddly, there hadn't been much snow. Decembers were always iffy in terms of snowfall. Sometimes there was a white Christmas, sometimes not. January typically brought plenty of storms, but this year seemed to be an exception. So far, there were only dustings of an inch or two. It appeared that the weather gods were making up for that by bringing in the subzero temperatures instead.

When she reached the museum, she glanced out across the harbor. It looked nearly frozen in again. It was a strange sight, a long, gray, very flat surface that suddenly connected two land masses which had been long separated by water. It wouldn't last, however. The ice breaker would come through it again, chopping a path for boats to use as they came and went. There were always boats in the harbor. Granted, far fewer during the winter months, but some still braved the cold. It was Maine after all. A true Yankee couldn't let a little thing like below zero temperatures stop the general industry.

Dulcie unlocked the museum door with some difficulty as she did not want to take off her gloves. She pushed it open and felt a blast of heat hit her. Now she pulled off her gloves, pressed the security code on the keypad, and heard the inner door lock click. She leaned against the heavy glass door and went inside.

In her office it took a good ten minutes to slide off all of her outer layers, change into her shoes, fix her hair, and make sure she was somewhat presentable. Her assistant, Rachel, tapped on the doorframe and popped her head in. "Enjoy the stroll in this morning?" she quipped.

"Holy cow!" Dulcie replied. "If that doesn't wake me up, nothing will!"

Rachel giggled "How about some coffee? I was just getting some. Then we can go over the setup for the new exhibit."

"Have I ever told you that you're an angel?" Dulcie said.

"I'm just a morning person," Rachel laughed. "Be right back." She scooted out of the room.

"And I am, most decidedly, not," Dulcie muttered to herself. She took her laptop out of her bag and flipped it open on her desk. First she glanced through her calendar, then quickly flicked through email, pausing to read a few messages, but deleting most. Somehow the spam filter never seemed to catch everything. She was just about to close the computer when a familiar name popped up.

"Huh!" Dulcie exclaimed, sitting back in her chair.

"Huh, what?" asked Rachel, walking back in with coffee and her own laptop under her arm.

"Huh!" Dulcie said again, then looked up at her assistant. "It seems that my old boyfriend from Oxford is coming to town. He wants to have lunch with me."

"Oooohhhhh!" Rachel hooted. "And how will the new beau handle that, I wonder?"

"With poise and decorum, I'm sure. Things have been decidedly over for a long time with Mr. Brendan MacArthur," Dulcie replied.

She and Portland police detective Nicholas Black had recently begun dating. They had agreed go slowly. Nick had initiated the relationship, or at least inadvertently revealed his feelings for her, before ending a previous attachment. It didn't exactly make him appear to be the most trustworthy person in Dulcie's eyes. She knew that there had been circumstances to explain the entire situation, and everyone else seemed to think that she was making far too much of it, but still. She had always trusted her instincts, and they were always right. Well, they were right most of the time.

Rachel was still talking. "I'm sorry, I wasn't listening. What did you just say?" Dulcie asked.

Rachel snickered. "You're sure things are over? You looked pretty lost just then!" She put up her hand to stop Dulcie's retort. "Okay, okay! Yes, I'm sure they are. But what's up? What brings him here?"

"I don't know," Dulcie said. "He says he's been working on a project and would love to talk with me about it."

"An art project?" Rachel replied.

"I can't imagine it would be. Brendan was never really interested in art. It was one of the many things that we did not have in common. He became an archaeologist, but I don't think it was to learn about antiquities necessarily. The thrill of the hunt seemed far more interesting to him. Once he'd located a site, he seemed less interested and mostly left it up to others to do the excavation. I remember that when we parted ways, he had begun to look for shipwrecks. Last I heard he'd been all over the world with a diving crew. They actually found a few minor wrecks I think."

"Wow, that's pretty exciting," said Rachel. "But really expensive I'd think. How'd he get the money, I wonder? Grants? University funds?" Rachel could always be counted on to bring practicality into any conversation.

Dulcie smiled. "That was another thing about Brendan. He was never lacking in funds. He came from money, family money. He could pretty much do whatever he wanted."

"Must be nice," Rachel mused. "So what did you two have in common?"

Dulcie took a deep breath. What they did have in common was something nearly as ancient as mankind. Something that, at its peak of perfection, was almost indescribable. They had even travelled around Europe hoping to find the hidden and elusive flawless vintage.

"Wine," Dulcie said simply. "What we had in common was wine."

ᘓ

Detective Nicholas Black looked up from his desk as a shadow loomed over him. "Hey! You're back!" he grinned.

"That I am," answered detective Adam Johnson. He lumbered around his partner and sat down in his battered chair behind the desk facing Nick's.

"And looking very svelte, might I add!" Nick exclaimed.

"Hey, no comments from the peanut gallery!" Johnson growled. "I won that bet fair and square. I just chose to go to the weight loss center. Figured I could learn a thing or two."

Johnson had spent an agonizing month trying to lose weight after making a bet with his wife. If she won, he would go to a weight loss center for a week. If he won, he would go to the Boston Red Sox baseball spring training camp in Florida and see them play, "While eating all the sausages I want!" he never failed to mention.

"You won but you still went to the spa? Are you crazy?" Nick was surprised.

"Well, here's how it went down. I lost the ten pounds, so I won the bet. But when I went back to the doctor, he said I was still about ten pounds into the 'obese' category. If I lost another ten, I'd merely be in the 'overweight' category. I can live with overweight, but obese just made it sound gross."

"Literally," said Nick. He eyed his partner. "Ya know, now that you mention it, you have lost some weight. Did it help with the snoring?"

Adam Johnson's wife, Maria, had complained bitterly about his snoring, prompting the initial visit to the doctor. He had objected of course, but was summarily overruled by his wife. Adam had expected to hear that the snoring was normal and nothing could be done. After all, everyone in Johnson's entire family snored like a freight train. But the doctor said that it was because Johnson was overweight, or rather, 'obese' as he had put it. Thinking about it, Johnson realized that pretty much all of his family could fall into that category too. They were a group of hearty eaters. When Maria heard this, she instigated the bet.

"Maria says it has, but how do I know? I mean, I'm asleep, right?"

"Good point," Nick chuckled. "So no Sox games at spring training camp?"

Johnson stared at him for a moment. "Are you joking? Of course I'm still doing that! I mean, I won the bet!"

"So I'll have to learn to live without you for another week in April," said Nick. "How will I ever face it?"

Johnson threw a crumpled wad of paper at his partner. "Oops. Sorry. Aiming for the trash can."

Nick grabbed it off the floor and flicked it across the room, into the trash. "Yeah, it's over there numbskull."

Johnson ignored him. "So what did I miss?" he asked.

Nick rolled his eyes. "A whole lotta nuthin," he answered. "Seriously, not a single case. I've resorted to going back through the cold files. Care to hear about any of them?"

"If I say 'No' will it make any difference?" Johnson asked.

"Probably not," Nick said. "But job security, after all. Have to stay busy."

"Let's stay busy and go get a coffee," Johnson suggested.

"Uh, you do realized it's like a hundred below out?" Nick replied.

"Yeah, but you burn more calories in the cold! See, I learned that at fat camp!"

"I don't think I need to burn more calories right now," Nick said.

"Johnson stood up and started putting on the coat he'd slung over the back of his chair. "Yeah, you think that now, but you just wait another ten years. The ol' metabolism slows down and you start packing on the pounds before you know it. Best to get into good habits as early as you can!"

"I'm not sure I like the new and improved Johnson," grumbled Nick.

"Yes you do! Of course you do! Now get your lazy butt out of that seat and c'mon." He was already heading toward the door, pulling on a black knit hat that made him look unnervingly like a bank robber.

Nick shook his head, sighed and, grabbing his own coat, followed Johnson out the door.

CB

Brendan MacArthur stood in the tiny cabin of the fishing boat he had rented and peeled off his dry suit. One other crew member was doing the same beside him. The other two were on the bridge, steering the vessel back into Portland harbor.

Earlier in the fall Brendan had carried out methodical research to locate a clipper ship that had gone missing in 1869. He had even located the diary of a woman who, as a little girl, had lived on one of the farthest islands in Casco Bay. In one passage she recalled, "either something real or something I dreamt that looked quite like the mast of a ship with tattered sails amongst huge crashing surf." Brendan knew that people who lived by the ocean had a far different definition of 'huge crashing surf' than those who did not. If this girl said the waves were huge, then they must have been monsters.

Brendan was thorough. He had found as much information as he could on the woman. He also checked weather records for 1869. There was one major culprit that had slammed into Maine's coast: the Saxby Gale. It had taken place in October. The woman's diary recalled that the event had happened in the fall of that year. He carefully pieced together the facts which led him to one conclusion: there was a 19th century shipwreck off the tip of Cliff Island at a location known as Johns Ledge.

Why hadn't anyone else found it? Maybe the woman had dreamt the whole thing as a little girl. Maybe it wasn't really there. Maybe it had broken up to the extent that there was nothing left. Maybe it was covered with so much debris and seaweed that nobody recognized it as a ship.

Or maybe no one had bothered to look.

Brendan had been very excited, but he had to contain every ounce of it. He was part archaeologist, part treasure hunter. He knew from experience that only extremely trustworthy people could be told about this possibility. And given that Johns Ledge was relatively close to Cliff Island, now inhabited by quite a few people, he didn't want to be observed there either.

He called together his closest group of colleagues. They couldn't exactly be called friends, but they had at least two common interests: scuba diving and treasure hunting. They were all too willing to look at the site.

The four men had planned two exploratory dives, one in September and one in October. Brandan was careful to rent a different boat each time. To the average onlooker, the men would appear to be just another group of recreational divers.

Ironically, it was during the October dive that they had found it, nestled into the ledge about 24 feet down. They had located it at the end of the dive and had little air left. They stayed down as long as they could, using up every last ounce in their tanks.

As a trained archaeologist, Brendan knew that he probably would be able to oversee the excavation. The site would have to be made known to the state. But not quite yet. Brendan had to think about his next move. He had to plan carefully. He was very good at that.

His fellow divers were not as excited about the site. An initial inspection showed them that it really didn't contain anything valuable. The ship had hauled goods for trade that would have brought in a very high profit at the time, but were worth little now.

Brendan decided that one more dive was needed. A winter dive. It was dangerous at that time of year, but Cliff Island had far fewer people on it in the winter. All of the seasonal cottages would be closed up tight. He and his crew could get down to the wreck and bring up a few things 'off the record.' Then he would officially announce the find, register it, and start the actual 'boring archaeology bit' as he called it.

They had pulled up a couple of crates with porcelain dishes when Brendan found something which was potentially of great value that the others had missed. He had located a crate of bottles and they appeared to be full of wine. He had replaced the bottle that he had pulled out quickly. No one else had seen them. The others would find out eventually, but he wanted to learn as much as he could before they did. It would give him an advantage, and Brendan certainly knew how to make good use of an advantage.

With his dry suit off and jeans, heavy socks, boots, sweater, jacket… all of the other layers needed to brave the freezing air now on, Brendan turned to his crewmate. "So, Alan looks like not much."

"Yeah," Alan replied. "Some of the cargo was packed well though. Could be unbroken porcelain dishes and such. Collectors like that stuff. Could get some bucks for that."

Technically, anything as old as this wreck found in coastal waters belonged to the government. But Brendan and his colleagues had to make a living. They helped themselves to a few things first before announcing any new find. When it was time to sell the items, "I found it in grandma's attic," was always an excellent provenance.

Brendan was careful to be sure that the pieces they helped themselves to were more commonplace; nothing of great value or significance could be taken outright. It wasn't that he cared about their place in history, he just didn't want to get caught.

"True. Worth bringing those few crates up I suppose." Brendan said. "I'll have to set up a grid and record some things too, once we're done getting our share. Have to keep the authorities happy." As soon as he made the wreck known, funding would come in to analyze it. He'd never had much of a problem with that. It was bread and butter money for him and his colleagues. Enough to pay the regular bills, but not much extra.

The archaeological part was tedious work. He hoped that a PhD candidate would step forward to take on the project. They almost always did. Then Brendan could move on to the next search.

"What about that wine?"

Brendan froze, then frowned. He hadn't realized that Alan had seen it. "Must have turned by now. Can't keep even the best of that stuff for more than half a century or so, I think," Brendan lied. "That wine has to be at least 150 years old down there." He shrugged. "The bottles themselves might have some value. Worth bringing up I guess." He motioned toward the boat's bridge overhead. "You coming up?" he asked, trying to change the subject as quickly as possible. It worked.

"Nah," Alan responded. "Too crowded up there. I think I'll just take a short nap. We've got probably half an hour or so before we're back in, yeah?" He didn't wait for an answer. He was already adjusting the life preservers to create a reasonably comfortable bed.

Brendan chuckled to himself. Alan always had been the lazy one.

If you would like to read more of LAST OF THE VINTAGE, please visit the author's web site (kerryjcharles.com) for more information, or request it at your local bookstore. Ebook versions are available from major suppliers online.

Reviews from thoughtful readers are always welcome on any website or media outlet. Thank you!

ABOUT THE AUTHOR

Kerry J Charles has worked as a researcher, writer, and editor for *National Geographic*, the Smithsonian Institution, Harvard University and several major textbook publishers. She holds four degrees including a Masters in Geospatial Engineering and a Masters in Art History from Harvard University. She has carried out research in many of the world's art museums as a freelance writer and scholar.

A swimmer, scuba diver, golfer, and boating enthusiast, Charles enjoys seeing the world from above and below sea level as well as from the tee box. Her life experiences inspire her writing and she is always seeking out new travels and adventures. She returned to her roots in coastal Maine while writing the Dulcie Chambers Museum Mysteries.